A COWARD'S CHRONICLES

A COWARD'S CHRONICLES

Marti Caine

ARROW BOOKS

Arrow Books Limited
20 Vauxhall Bridge Road, London SW1V 2SA

An imprint of the Random Century Group

London Melbourne Sydney Auckland Johannesburg
and agencies throughout the world

First published in Great Britain by Century 1990
Arrow edition 1991

Printed and bound in Great Britain by
Courier International Ltd, Tiptree, Essex

ISBN 0 09 971490 6

For Mr Lowe

Preface

Oh, my God! It says here I'm brave. (**Well, it must be true if it's in the papers.**) But I'm not brave, I'm afraid. I'm going to die. God help me, I'm going to die. (**Get a grip on yourself, woman.**)

It says here that '25 per cent of the population die of cancer'. (**And you're just another statistic, but you *are* in a position to help others.**)

How can I help? (**By writing a success story to inspire other fighters.**)

I'll do it! It'll help me to stay positive. I can see it now: *A Hero's Handbook.*

(**More like *A Coward's Chronicles*.**)

1

Monday 3 October 1988 – 4.30 p.m.
Dr Newcombe's consulting room, Harley Street

He looked down at the copious notes in front of him and cleared his throat again. I remained impassively seated, surrounded by what I hoped was an air of calm composure. (**Think it and you'll be it.**) 'Well, Mrs Ives!' The eyes flickered up to meet mine for a split second before returning to his notes. I already knew. An urgent giggle worked its way up through my sphincter muscles and caught in my throat. (**Stay calm, stay calm, control it!**)

I giggled when my Mother died. I was standing in the mortuary, flanked by two policemen, looking down at her. It wasn't really her, just a wax effigy, a place where she used to be.

She hardly made a bump under the sheet, only her small shaven head and long neck were visible. Her beautiful profile was etched against the clinical white-tiled wall behind, hiding the hideously scarred right side of her face from instant view.

A firm, insistent hand between my shoulder-blades pushed me further into the room; my feet moved, but my body refused to follow and I realised I was standing at an angle.

'Is this Elizabeth Young Laurie Fisher, aged 42 years?'

'Yes, it's her,' I giggled.

'The biopsy confirms that you have a malignant lymphoma.'

Silence!

'Does this mean I'm a lymphomaniac?' I was hoping he'd laugh and so allow my giggle a justifiable release. He didn't. He blinked and regarded me with confused surprise.

'No!' he said earnestly. I smiled. **(Not as good as a giggle, but at least it's relieved his embarrassment.)**

'There are many different types of lymphoma, but basically they can be divided into two groups, aggressive and non-aggressive. You have a variety which is treatable – but not curable.'

'Yes, but will I ever play the violin again?'

'Pardon!?'

(He thinks you've cracked up under the strain – ask him about his geraniums.)

'Those geraniums out there look marvellous!'

'They're pelargoniums.'

'Ah!'

We exchanged small talk while he examined the armpit bearing the small neat scar from the recent biopsy. I complimented him on his artistic prowess as a surgeon; he smiled. **(At last! Go for the laugh!)**

'Did you always want to be an armpit specialist?'

He stopped smiling. 'Not at all, I'm a general surgeon.'

I wanted to ask, 'How long have I got?' but it's such a cliché. I wanted to see a lymph gland. (know thine enemy) I wanted to know everything there was to know about lymphoma, but I decided to save the questions – and the wit – for my own doctor who has an excellent sense of humour. (He'd have to with a name like Dingle.) The surgeon fixed an appointment with a leading oncologist and chemotherapist, Dr McKenzie, at 6.30 at the Cromwell Hospital tomorrow. (You've got a 'T.V.am' at 9 o'clock in Nottingham and a cheque presentation at 12 noon in Coventry – you could get back by 5 pm.)

It was 4.55 when I left his consulting room. My stilettos made a clip-thunk noise along the black and white marbled hallway leading to the door. (Damn! You've lost a heel – it'll look like a little upside-down palm tree by the time you get home.) Home! Kenneth! How am I going to tell him? We had both been convinced that the biopsy results would be benign.

Finding a taxi at 4.55 in London is every bit as possible as finding Bruce Willis in your bed. (Well, you can assess the situation while you're walking.) Bruce Willis screeched to a halt right outside. (You can assess the situation on the drive home). A talkative Bruce Willis dropped me outside the London flat fifteen minutes later (you can assess the situation on the way upstairs), and Kenneth came down to meet me at the door. (Who needs to assess the situation?)

There was five minutes of coat removal, coffee-making and slipper-finding, and a brief post mortem on my stiletto heel while the question burned unasked. (He's trying to read you. Put the poor sod out of his misery.) 'Did you water the plants?' (Coward.)

'What did the doctor say?'

I told him.

'Oh!' said his mouth.

'Scream' said his eyes. 'How do you feel?' continued his mouth. (**How DO you feel?**) 'Well, nothing like I'd imagined I'd feel in this situation.' (**Gazing out of the window during Mr Battersby's history lesson. What would you do if:**

A) **You won £1,000,000?**
B) **The Russians invaded Rotherham?**
C) **You'd only got six months to live?**)

'As a matter of fact, I feel excited (**that's the spirit!**), like it's the beginning of a new chapter, a new freedom, what have I got to lose? The shackles are off, so go for it! I'm so glad to be alive. I don't want to miss a second of it. It's funny but life seems infinitely sweeter (**you're going over the top now**); anyway I thrive on challenges and this is the ultimate one. I don't intend to die, and that's that!' (**God, woman — you're such a drama queen. You see yourself as the mysterious contessa in flowing black veil and wheelchair, delicate white hand with long red nails offered up for kissing.**)

Practical things had to be discussed. How and when to tell the kids, Malc, Pam, Rog, my agent? Should I tell Central T.V.? I have the final of '**New Faces**' coming up, followed by the pantomime and oh God!, the hyperbole of the press. How long can I keep it a secret? My job is to raise laughs and cancer is hardly conducive. I still feel as fit as a butcher's dog; if I confine the news to my close circle, perhaps I can keep it out of the press. (**You're kidding yourself, girl!**) My kids aren't aware that anything is wrong. Pam and Malc, being my soul-mates, know everything there is to know about me.

Pam was there from the beginning, or at least from the first day of school. We were born on the same council estate – Shiregreen, in Sheffield, both 'well off by council house standards (first with a telly and matching frocks and knickers).

We both had a doll and pram when we were seven and the real thing ten years later. She held my hand when my dad died and my coat when I fought with Margaret Scholey. We've bailed each other out and bolstered each other up, we know without asking, so it would have been pointless trying to hide it from her when I first discovered the lumps eighteen months ago.

Malc is my ex-husband, we were married when we were 17 – (just) and after 18 years were divorced to a chorus of, 'I knew it wouldn't last!' They were 18 of the best and worst years of our lives. We grew together struggling for supremacy like a wisteria – two trunks from one root – twining tortuously round each other's faults and failings and culminating in the glorious flowers of two fine sons and a deep and immovable friendship.

During my annual medical check-up in 1987, Dr Dingle discovered a blood irregularity, but as I was fighting fit he said it was probably just a virus and I was to forget about it during my impending holiday and to see him on my return for a second blood test.

At the beginning of our second week in Corfu, I woke up to find a lump beneath my left arm the size of a pigeon's egg and two smaller ones running into my breast.

Panic!

Breast cancer – I was sure of it, hence the blood irregularity. Like everyone else, I'd played the 'It won't happen to me, but if it does . . .' game, and had envisaged, in the case of breast cancer, dying intact, yet there I was, rushing round the taverna looking for a scalpel.

I didn't mention it to Kenneth initially as I didn't want to spoil his holiday, but my martyrdom was brief and his subsequent concern touching. **(He carried the beach mats for the rest of the week.)**

On returning home, Dr Dingle reassured me. The large lump was a swollen gland – probably the result of the blood irregularity which, according to the second test, had now returned to normal. As for the smaller lumps running into my breast, it was just fibrous tissue which would go away. I *felt* incredibly well, but he said to keep an eye on the swollen gland and to see him immediately if it grew in size. As predicted, the small lumps vanished, the gland remained – unchanged – and after a few weeks, I grew accustomed to the feel of it and forgot it until Dr Dingle rediscovered it during my 1988 medical. He also found two more lumps in my groin and immediately booked me into the Princess Grace Hospital for the biopsy I had five days ago.

The phone rang, it was Malc. 'What was the result of the biopsy?' I told him.

The phone rang, it was Pam. 'What was the result of the biopsy?' I told her.

Despite their almost identical chorus of 'Pah! Piece of cake for you girl, if anyone can beat it you can, you're a survivor, a fighter etc.', I knew they were as devastated and shocked as Kenneth. **(Without a doubt the worst thing so far is telling those you love. It's much harder on them than it is on you.)**

It's 1.30 a.m. and I should go to bed, long day tomorrow. I'll have to catch the 7 a.m. train to Notting-

ham, which means getting up at 5 a.m. to put the slap on
and climb into the overalls. I'm too excited to sleep. Life
has taken on a new sense of urgency and my mind is
working overtime. (Anyone would think you'd been
offered the leading role in the latest Spielberg epic, for
God's sake, you're supposed to be depressed or something. Maybe tomorrow it will hit you.) There's so
much to do. I'll start by counting my blessings.

*My life, which began on January 26th 1945, has been full of
blessings. My Father, a shy gentle man, was with the Eighth
Army Medical Corps in Scotland when he met and married my
Mother. She was highly strung and beautiful and had never been
away from her large family or Plean – the mining village where
she was born.*

*My paternal Grandfather was a stubborn, domineering man
who intimidated my little Grandmother and everyone else.
(You're just like him.) He never really accepted my Mother, who
had the temerity to marry his son, but was nonetheless as over-
joyed as my parents when, after four years, I was conceived.*

*When my Mother went into labour, it was he and not my
Grandmother who performed the midwifery until the ambulance
arrived, then ran behind it shouting, 'Make it a girl, Betty, make
it a girl.'*

*He dedicated himself to me. He secured a council house for
my parents, with a garden that butted up to his own, and I enjoyed a sublime if insular childhood, basking in the adoration of
my shy parents and doting grandparents.*

*Every evening at 6.30, my 'Pop', as I called him, would
come across the garden to take me to bed and read me a story.
He didn't approve of smoking or drinking and my Dad was so
dominated by him that he would hide his pipe behind a cushion –
once setting fire to the chair – for fear of incurring his wrath.*

With me, however, Pop was soft and over-indulgent and the evening ritual never varied. Hands behind his back he'd ask, 'Which hand?'

Whichever I chose would be empty and I'd wait, wide-eyed with disappointment, till with a flourish he produced a small toy or sweets from behind his back.

A sawdust-scented hug, then a piggy-back up the stairs: 'Who's my little angel?'

'I am.'

'And how many sugars do you love me?'

'A million pounds.' And he'd bounce me on my bed and make a 'little nest' by tucking the ends of the eiderdown under my pillow until all but my face was cocooned.

Over and over again he would read out my favourite stories, sometimes with deliberate mistakes for me to correct. I knew Little Black Sambo and Brer Rabbit and the Tar Baby by heart, and among my other favourites were The Water Babies, Wind in the Willows, Alice in Wonderland and Treasure Island.

He was foreman pattern-maker at the English Steel Corporation and he taught woodwork at night school. He would make beautiful toys for me at work, smuggling the pieces out in his wooden case to be reassembled at home.

A wooden scooter he'd made tipped me over the handlebars on its maiden voyage and he picked it up and smashed it to smithereens against a lamp-post, as if it were a cobra that had just delivered a fatal bite.

A wooden Scotty-dog with a waggly, leather jointed body nipped my finger, and he snatched it from me and hurled it on to the fire, hitting it repeatedly with the poker until it disintegrated.

He made me a desk with a roll-top and secret drawers and a matching leather stool; a huge Tudor doll's house with leaded windows and roses round the door, filled with hand-carved furniture; a bow-windowed shop with a sign saying 'Lynne's Store'

and shelves stocked with dozens of tiny tins of Heinz products –
it had taken him a year to cut out all the miniature Heinz logos
from magazine adverts, which he had stuck to one-inch lengths
of silver-painted dowelling.

My favourite was a Wendy house which he'd furnished with
a tiny drop-leaf mahogany table, two matching chairs and a T.V.
with clicking knobs and a picture of the Queen behind the per-
spex screen.

On Tuesdays, Dad took me to the children's cinema, on
Wednesdays, Pop took me to Sally Carmichael's dancing class,
and on Saturdays my Nan would take me to the variety show at
the Sheffield Empire. I was the centre of their universe and my
first seven years sped by in a whirl of buckskin shoes, party
frocks, pet rabbits and circus trips.

My parents were besotted with each other and always in
each other's arms. Our home was full of laughter and love, Dick
Barton and the Billy Cotton Band Show, crisp sheets and shiny
furniture. I was coddled and cosseted, pampered and petted and
never shouted at.

I was naughty sometimes. I once took all eleven of my Dad's
angel fish to school in a jam-jar and poured them into the pond
to keep the goldfish company.

Once, when he was asleep in his chair, I decided to trim the
hairs on my Dad's legs with my Mom's dressmaking scissors and
took a chunk out of his leg with my first snip.

I was only smacked once, a fiery look from my Mother
being sufficient deterrent for most mischief. It was a Saturday.
We had a Morris 8, and my Dad would drive me and Mom into
the town centre to do the week-end shopping. My Mother loved
being a big-city girl. She developed an eye for fashion and an air
of glamour and all heads would turn as we walked along.

She had affected what she considered a posh English accent
and I'd die with embarrassment in the French pastry shop when,

pointing with her little finger, she'd say; 'Emm! I'll take wanni these and wanni those and wanni they whey the wee silver baw's on.'

This particular Saturday I'd been allowed – for the first time – to stay at home alone. Dad and Pop had built a garage and had just finished laying a concrete drive. It was the pride of the council estate. It had hardened without foot- or paw-print and stretched pale and virginal up the side of the house, the only imperfection being a small superfluous 'tab' where a sliver of wet cement had oozed through the battening.

I thought I'd remove it and, taking a hammer from the tool-shed, lightly tapped the offending projection. A crack the size of the Grand Canyon streaked up the drive, stopping only when it reached the garage doors.

I got my just desserts from Dad, which made my Mom cry more than me, but all in all I was given enough love and affection to cushion me against all the hardships that were to come.

Five a.m. and still counting. I'll tell you what! I'm a lucky girl, I've got nothing to whinge about. Even if I die **(which we won't)** life has been wonderful. I even enjoyed the bad times in retrospect.

Strange how what you regard at the time as being your downfall, often turns out to be the making of you. Ah, well – on with the motley.

Tuesday 4 October – 5 p.m.
St Pancras Station

A successful day! 'TV.am' went OK. I like Mike Scott. I didn't meet him in person as it was a studio link-up. Nina Myskow was on the show – wish we'd have been together, we bounce off each other so well. **(You must tell Nina.)** I'll tell her when the opportunity presents itself. It doesn't seem right on the phone (**. . . must dash, oh, by the way, I'm dying).** She's a good friend.

The Candis presentation went well too. **(You can't fail when you're handing over a cheque for £50,000.)** Kenneth is meeting me, to drive me to the Cromwell Hospital. **(Very posh – Gucci bandages!)** I might have known, Pam and Malc are there as well. They've driven down from Sheffield to come with me. **(The gang's all here! Like a brick wall to protect you. A net to catch you if you fall – you're right, you are a lucky girl!).** God, I love them all so much, I hate being the cause of their distress.

But if the while I think of thee, dear friend
All losses are restored and sorrows end. Shakespeare

(You're so grandiose! That and the 'Good Ship Venus' are the only two sonnets you know.)

Pam hugged me and we scrutinised each other's wardrobe, as usual. This scrutinisation takes all of a split second. She had on a superb raspberry pink swagger coat. **(Probably £600 quids worth of Max Mara – you should seriously consider killing for it.)** It contrasted nicely with my black Escada twin-set and leather skirt. Malc struck his usual pose: hands in pockets, shoulders hunched, eyes peering over the top of his specs.

'Now then!' A hug!

Six feet four inches of Kenneth paces up and down behind us, muttering about time and traffic. We're early, so we call in at a pub. Kenneth leading the way, trench mac billowing, we running three steps to his one to keep up. Duck to the bar, ducklings panting to a seat. Pam drinks to match her outfit, today she's wearing vodka tonic. I remember Malc's rum punch days (**rum – and punch anything**) and his Yorkshire lad days (**14 pints, a black pudding and domino puke**); now he's matured to a steady G. & T. In the absence of Lucozade I order a Coke and Kenneth a beer, and after ten minutes of chat we leave for our appointment, promising to rejoin them later.

My first encounter with Dr McKenzie. He seems a nervous, gentle man, ill at ease in grey pinstripe, yet difficult to envisage dressed any other way. Thin smile, slight bow – almost an oriental attitude.

'Mr and Mrs Ives? Please step this way.' Quietly spoken. A beautiful Philippino nurse with a warm smile slid out of – as we slid into – a small office. We seated ourselves and he regarded us expectantly, so I opened with, 'Can you tell me all about lymphomas and can I see a lymph node?' He answered earnestly and in words I could understand. He did little drawings and explained without patronising. He recommended certain books. He was kind. I liked him. Kenneth liked him too and joined in the questioning. (**At last Kenneth is beginning to thaw. He's been paralysed with fear since you told him.**) I thought of a way of avoiding the cliché and asked, 'What is the average life expectancy of someone with follicular lymphoma?'

'Five years,' (**Kenneth's back in deep-freeze**), 'but I would expect you to do better.' (**How does LIVE FOR EVER grab you, doc?**) 'We'll know more after a scan and a bone-marrow expiration!' An appointment is made for October 10th.

2

Today is Paul Daniels' 'This is Your Life' and I'm a surprise guest. A car is picking me up at 1.30 to take me to Thames T.V. to be made up as a Chinese coolie. That's all I know.

I first met Paul in the Working Men's Club days of twenty-odd years ago in Sunderland. He was a local lad and already a star in clubland, and I was a second-year apprentice comic visiting the north-east for the first time and decidedly wary of its reputation. Among my more experienced colleagues, the north-east was known as 'Calvary' as most acts were crucified there. Malc and I would listen in horror to gruesome tales of evil committee men, savage audiences and dreadful pro-digs – along with the latest Freddie Starr folklore. The north-east was no place to refine one's art, but the money was good (if you could prise it from the agent) and it widened my working circle (if you survived.) So we finally succumbed.

Malc's parents moved into our house to look after Lee and Max and loaded with amps, speakers and suitcases, we set off for the first of twelve gigs – a Sunday lunch, one spot, fourteen quid – money for old rope.

We arrived at the club with minutes to spare. My heart stopped. Newly flung mashed potato clung to the walls, testament to what the Rugby Supporters' Club thought of the 'mash' part of the lunch. The 'bangers' part was being utilised by a large-breasted naked lady who was on stage gyrating to a trio, barely audible above the cat-calls and jeers of the all-male audience. They were animals.

Malc was behind me with a speaker on each shoulder. 'Don't make any sudden moves, girl, just back out slowly.' The words died on his lips as an enormous red-faced committee man appeared and blocked the door.

'Are you the comic?' he asked Malc.

'No, it's her,' said Malc (before the cock crowed thrice).

The man looked disbelievingly and laughed: 'Christ! I hope you can sing pet, they're not always this polite.' I nodded. 'What kind of songs do you sing?'

'Folk'n'ballads.'

'There's no call for that kind of language. Follow me, you're on after Tanya's finished. It should have been Princess Voluptua, but her car's broken down, so I'll have to put you on or they'll get rowdy.'

The carpet sucked the soles of our shoes as we followed him through a drunken, grasping audience towards a small dressing room to the left of the stage, upon which Tanya was enjoying bananas for desert.

'How long is her spot?' I shouted above the noise.

'You've got about five minutes. She hasn't done the tennis balls yet.' Interested curiosity replaced the look of fear on Malc's

face and for a moment I hated him. Once behind the closed door of the dressing room we looked for a way out, but there wasn't one.

'Best get on, get off and get out, love,' said Malc gently, and went off to watch Tanya dispose of the tennis balls, leaving me to climb into my home-made stage gear.

Tanya finished to a burst of indifference as a hand bearing a microphone was thrust through the curtain that separated the lions from the Christians.

'Take the mike, give us your dots, you've got an eight-bar play on, then it's every man for himself. What's your name?'

'Marti Caine.'

'Right. You're on!'

Shaking and belching with fear, I took the microphone and wondered vaguely if Tanya had used it and how. I caught sight of myself in the peeling mirror: long thin legs, blue from the cold, clashing with the bright pink mini-dress which began at my neck and finished at my knickers. The design of the dress robbed me of breasts but revealed white angular shoulders which added an extra foot to my thin white arms. I looked like a rag doll, and they were expecting Princess Voluptua.

I waited a thousand years for my introduction, then the curtains opened and I found myself centre-stage. A stunned silence fell upon the room as they focused their attention on what they thought was Princess Voluptua.

To survive, a performer has to establish dominance within twenty seconds, and already I could feel the pack instinct rising in them. 'Ger 'em off!' slurred one, to the amusement of his fellows.

'If it's as big as your mouth, you're on,' I replied with a cool nonchalance that belonged to someone else (that was me, you fool!). The retort earned a laugh and gave me a split second to stop my heart from racing.

'We want tits,' yelled another.

'You'd look bright sparks with tits,' I said as though I didn't have a nerve in my body, and the audience were mine.

Oh, the power! I dangled and titillated them, controlled and manipulated them. Even Tanya stayed to watch, standing at the back of the room draped in fake ocelot, with the glow of her Woodbine reflected in her lip-gloss.

By the time I worked with Paul, three days later, word had spread and his first words were, 'Marti Caine, I've heard you're good, but blue.' (He must have heard about your legs!)

Two other unlikely 'coolies' were already in make-up having the final touches applied; one was Bert Weedon, the other Duncan Goodhew – both good-natured souls. The make-up girl went to work on me as Duncan and I reminisced about the last time we'd worked together.

It was during the filming of the opening titles for the last 'Marti' series for the B.B.C. Dressed in a red chiffon evening gown, high heels and lead-weighted knickers, I had to sit on a rock at the bottom of a tank full of sharks, smiling and brushing my hair, while Duncan swam past with a plywood plaice bearing the immortal words 'End of Part One' (it could have been the end of several parts!). Stuart Morris – the producer – an expansive, explosive man, was furious when, despite the weighted knickers, I kept floating to the surface of the tank.

He screamed abuse. The sharks seemed less intimidating, so I gulped a lung-full of air and flapped like crazy in an effort to regain my position at the bottom of the tank, clutching my hair-brush and trying to control miles of floating red chiffon. By the time I got into position, my lungs were bursting and I had to go up for air again. The problem was finally solved by fixing a wire to my ankle and running it under the rock to an aqua-lunged diver, who on a signal from Stuart would tug on the wire and pull me down with the speed of an express lift, and would let go when my face turned blue. The water was very cold, it took eight hours to film and eight days for Duncan's head to lose that 'prune' look.

Bert and Duncan were as uninformed as I regarding the forthcoming events of the programme. If the subject finds out he or she is being 'done', the programme is cancelled. They got me in 1979 when Eamonn Andrews hosted the show. I had absolutely no idea and put Malc's brief disappearances and inexplicable whispered phone calls down to the fact that he was being unfaithful to his mistress. I had secretly harboured a vague desire to be a subject (**Vague desire?! You used to stay in every Wednesday to see if it was you!**), and was delighted by the accolade. I hoped Paul would be.

Just as my make-up was finished an old mandarin shuffled in, slit-eyed and moustached, and said, 'Hello' in Michael Aspel's voice. He was quite unrecognisable. He explained the set-up; Duncan and I were to pull an Aspel-laden rickshaw through the busy streets of Char-ing Cross – ignoring the irate rush-hour traffic, which was being held up by an army of floor assistants – to the steps of Charing Cross underground station. From there we had to shuffle down the underground to Davenports Magic Shop, where Paul had been lured in order to buy an ancient Chinese trick, hence the coolie gear.

It's a wonderful shop, with a little theatre at the back to demonstrate various rare feats of magic to in-terested parties. For James – Pam's 7-year-old son – I bought several 'beginner's tricks' plus a plastic dog turd that steams when you fill it with hot water. (James will love it – Pam will never speak to you again!)

Duncan, Bert and I were to secrete ourselves behind the curtains along with Aspel, who was to demonstrate the trick with the help of his three 'assistants'. Paul came in and didn't seem at all surprised by the theatrics when the curtains opened revealing the four of us. He didn't recognise Aspel until the red book was produced from the wide sleeves of his costume and in his best mandarin accent he said, 'Paul Daniels – This Is Your Rife.'

The act of pulling the rickshaw tugged at the stitches in my armpit, the only reminder that I was a 'sick woman' (God, but you're a trooper), and the show went well.

I got home to find Kenneth hunched over his desk engrossed in a pile of newly purchased books on the subject of lymphoma and a medical dictionary to help him understand the terminology. Personally I couldn't even understand the titles, but Kenneth is a tenacious (not to say obsessive) man once he gets the bit between his teeth. He is determined to learn everything there is to learn about the subject.

Thursday 6 October

I have an appointment with Dr Dingle at 5 o'clock, so it seemed pointless going back to the Oxfordshire cottage last night. I don't like the London flat much. London is dirty and keeping the Edwardian terrace flat clean is a full-time job. The ceilings are about 16 feet high and cleaning the windows is foolhardy without a safety-net. Fixing the window leather to the broom, I stand on a bar stool on top of Kenneth's desk, and proceed with caution. (Wonder what Shirley Bassey's doing today?)

I've always loved cleaning, it helps me to think and stops me getting ideas above my station. When I was a tot, I had one of those Ewbank carpet sweepers. I wore out four carpets a year.

My Mom was very house-proud until my Dad died of lung cancer at the age of 32, leaving a 28-year-old her and a 7-year-old me.

After his death, she had difficulty sleeping, so the doctor prescribed nembutal sleeping tablets. My Dad had been her only friend. She must have been desperately lonely especially with all her family up in Scotland. She sought oblivion, and one tablet a night quickly escalated to two, then three, then a couple in the morning, then four, until eventually she was taking them like sweeties. She had four or five doctors and as many aliases. Of course, it wasn't long before she was rumbled, so she packed up and returned to Scotland, taking me with her.

I was fiercely proud of Scotland, having been indoctrinated by glowing tales from my Mother, and felt that the land was mine by birthright. I would have defended it and its people to the death and was understandably disillusioned when, on my arrival, I was beaten to a pulp because of the Battle of Bannockburn in 1314. Even the teachers hated me; one – a Miss McKeller – found some reason to lay the strap across my hands every day, and within a month I was stammering so badly no one could understand a word I said.

The education system was so different: the two times table, for instance – same tune, different lyrics. Instead of one two is two; two twos are four; three twos are six, it was two ones are two; two twos are four; two threes are six etc. I retreated into my shell, being painfully shy in the first place. I missed my grandparents desperately and longed for Pam.

My Mom took a job as a nursing orderly in a mental hospital where sleeping pills and tranquillisers were easily obtainable. She had discovered that mixing them with whisky heightened their effect, and my beautiful, fiery Mother became a zombie. She lost her job after a few weeks and what little money my Dad had left quickly went on drugs and booze. She took to visiting Glasgow regularly, presumably to purchase fresh supplies.

I would spend hours cleaning the house and washing and ironing, as if scrubbing, polishing and filling the house with familiar clean smells would bring back Dick Barton days and cauterize my mother's wound.

Around my eighth birthday, I came home from school to find two women waiting for me. They informed me that my Mom had been taken into hospital and I was to be taken into care until she recovered. They had already packed a small suitcase and I was allowed to collect three of my favourite toys, a red handbag, a doll called Arthur and a leather-bound Bible in Pictures.

They sidestepped my anxious questions. No, she wouldn't be in hospital long; she had tummy-ache; the lady next door would look after Blackie the cat. I said a silent farewell to my beautiful Tudor doll's house, my gleaming two-wheeler Raleigh, my blackboard and desk, doll's pram and crib, my pink eiderdown and basket chair – all the remnants of a privileged childhood – and off we went.

The edges of the picture become fuzzy from then on. I remember some other kids, a girls' dorm, green-painted walls with a red border half-way up, a stiff roller-towel next to a wash-hand-basin, the scent of carbolic soap, hugs from a kind, laughing lady with large arms and the comforting smell of B.O., and a small, quiet, wiry man who always seemed to be sweeping and winking.

I don't know how long I stayed there, except days became weeks and the answer to my persistent 'When?' was an insistent

'Soon'. Eventually I gave up hope of ever seeing my Mom again, and stealing a penny from beneath a milk bottle, bought a platform ticket and stowed away in the goods wagon of a train bound – I thought – for Sheffield and my beloved Grandfather. The train was a slow one that stopped at every station and I was eventually discovered, clutching my red handbag and Arthur, in Carlisle where the train terminated.

The station staff plied me with Penguin biscuits and saucers of sweet tea in an attempt to discover my embarkation point, but the only information I would part with was my Grandfather's address and place of employment. Some hours later he came striding into the station-master's office to collect me. I vividly remember the familiar scent of sawdust that perfumed the first hug. I returned to Sheffield and Pam and didn't see Scotland or my Mom again for several years. After a while, though, I started receiving letters from her, and on Sunday evenings my Pop would take me to the phone booth, where at a prearranged time I would ring a phone booth in Scotland and talk to her for 3 minutes.

Umpteen journalists **(and Terry Wogan)** have described this period of my life as 'deprived'. Not so. I gained infinitely more than I lost from the experience. I learned to use humour against violence; when my back was against the wall and the bullies were bearing down, some inner voice would lash out with wit enough to take the wind from the sails of my antagonists. **(Why be beaten up for nothing when you can be beaten up for being a smart-arse?)** I learned to share and to give and to gain my own goals. In short, it gave me 'back-bone' **(which you may well break attempting to clean these windows).**

Dr Michael Dingle's surgery is on the third floor, reached by an impossibly small lift **(Kenneth has to do it** in two trips). The doors juddered open to reveal him waiting to greet us. I've only been ill once – in 1969 with 24-hour 'flu – so visiting surgeries is a novel experience (which is palling fast). He examines the biopsy scar, the lumps in my groin and a couple of new ones that have come up in my neck overnight, and comments on how fit I am. (You'll make a very healthy corpse.)

Kenneth has a list of questions to ask as a result of his reading, but the Dr has to admit that the subject is a highly complex one and that his knowledge is limited as he is a G.P. and not a specialist on the subject. He says Kenneth probably knows more about it than he does and is sure Dr McKenzie at the Cromwell Hospital will be able to answer any questions. He's delighted to find my spirits high, my blood pressure low and that apart from the lumps, I remain asymptomatic. We say goodbye and head for the cottage and a lazy weekend.

I have a fitting on Sunday for the 'New Faces' final – one gown with three jackets to ring the changes over the ninety minutes of live T.V. It's imperative that I do the show as I can't think of anyone who could step into the breach should I become ill. (What about Gary Wilmot?) Gary Wilmot could possibly do it as, like me, he was a contestant on the show and would therefore understand the awesome fear the contestants have to cope with. I love doing 'New Faces', but it's not a job many pros would take on. You have to take a back seat and be 'an unselfish performer', and very few successful acts or 'stars' are unselfish. I'm not patting myself on the back – it's a highly competitive business and one needs selfish, single-minded dedication to succeed, but because female comics were rare in my day, competition was negligible, and I was able to be generous. In fairness to Central T.V.,

I'll have to inform Richard Holloway, my producer, of my condition. If the worst comes to the worst, and I'm unable to continue, he'll have to have someone standing by to fill in for me.

I still haven't resolved the problem of how to tell my sons. My original idea of telling them together was a bad one. They're so different. I know exactly how they'll react – one will be emotional, the other will change the subject – and neither will appreciate being told in front of the other. (**You don't have to think about it for another fortnight.**) Max – the younger – works in Sheffield, but Lee is in the Royal Marine Commandos and his next leave is two weeks away.

3

Monday 10 October

Scan Day! Quite a simple procedure, the worst of it being a blue paper nightie that fastens down the back, exposing the cellulite to a firm-buttocked young operator. (**Console yourself with the certain knowledge that she too will have a dimpled bum in a couple of years!**) She smilingly explains that the scanner is a sort of lie-down X-ray and leads me to a narrow bed that slides inch by inch through what looks like a dry-cleaning machine. Deep breath, hold it, whirr, click, move up an inch, breathe again. Deep breath, hold it and so on until I'm photographed from neck to thigh. Twenty minutes later I'm dressed again and being directed to another department for the bone-marrow expiration.

Not so pleasant. A green paper nightie this time, and by now I don't give a damn about the cellulite. I lie on my side in foetal position, while an extremely competent young doctor administers a local anaesthetic into the base of my spine. I know I'm in trouble when the beautiful Philippino nurse I met in Dr McKenzie's consulting room takes my hand and says, 'Hold tight and scream if you want.' (Ye Gods! **What are they going to do to you?**) Enter the doctor once more, hiding something behind her back. 'What's that?' I ask. (**You're too nosy for your own good.**) She shows me. It looks like something a navvy might use to dig roads up – thin, hollow metal tube, about as thick as a size 10 knitting needle, with a gimlet-like plunger. (**Told you! Try to relax.**) I try to relax – everything is easier if you relax – as the young doctor pushes the tube into the green bone of my pelvic girdle, pausing every few seconds to ask if I'm O.K. I am. In fact, I feel nothing except the pushing. Gaining confidence now, I try to help by pushing towards her. There's a brief explosion of pain, a bit like biting on an exposed nerve, and it's all over. She shows me the marrow, which looks like thick dark blood, and the tiny sliver of bone she has removed. Both will be sent for analysis and the results should be ready this evening along with the results of the scan.

It's strange, but since being diagnosed the word CANCER seems to leap out of every magazine and newspaper. T.V. and radio devote entire programmes to the subject. Everyone seems to be talking about CANCER. I suppose it's always been there, but I hadn't noticed before. Like when a love affair breaks up and every song on the radio seems pertinent.

I climb into a taxi and head for Harvey Nichols to do some damage with the Barclaycard and the taxi driver tells me about his brother-in-law.

'Thirty-five, he is, and he's just been told he's not got long to live. Two kids, nice house, good business and now this happens. Cancer of the lymph glands, he's got. I can't get it off my mind, I mean, what would you do if somebody told you that, Marti?'

'Well, as a matter of fact . . . 'I begin and it all comes blurting out to a complete stranger. The coincidence is too much, I can't stop myself. I instantly regret my indiscretion and beg him to keep the news to himself. He's visibly shocked and promises – 'on my kid's life' – not to spill the beans. I believe him. He won't accept the fare.

It's 8 o'clock as Kenneth and I strut into Dr McKenzie's consulting room for the results of the tests. He smiles a hello, but his eyes only touch mine briefly, a disquieting sign. Several of my scan pictures are backlit against a screen, but mean nothing to my layman's eye. His back to us, he concentrates on the pictures and comes straight to the point.

'The bad news is it's extensive – neck, axilla, aorta, diaphragm, spleen, liver, groin, and there's a shadow on the ovaries. The good news is there's some doubt, but it doesn't look as if the bone marrow is affected yet.'

I get up from my seat and stand beside him. 'Show me, please.'

'Here,' he said,' these little white patches – here and here.' He points with enthusiasm like an amateur photographer showing his Greek holiday slides.

'What about my lungs?'

'Clear,' he says with a broad smile. (Ironic, you smoke like a chimney and the lungs are O.K.)

'I smoke, should I stop?'

'Your disease is not smoke related, and right now your equilibrium is important; you shouldn't give yourself any extra stress, but you should think about stopping.' I *think* about stopping every day; I've tried hypnosis, acupuncture, pills, potions, chewing-gum – even aversion therapy, where you get an electric shock every time you take a drag. **(Now you can't enjoy a fag without sticking your fingers in a three-point socket.)**

'How are you feeling generally?' he asks.

'Terrific,' I reply candidly.

'Well, I'll put you on a course of chlorambucil and you'll begin to feel better.' **(How can you feel better than terrific?)** If I stretch my imagination, I can admit to feeling a little tired lately, but put that down to the ageing process. I still have an abundance of energy that leaves my contemporaries standing. Dr McKenzie fills out a prescription and explains that chlorambucil is a mild chemotherapy tablet that may cause nausea. I'm to take one 10mg tablet daily for ten days, starting tomorrow, and the lumps on my body should begin to subside. **(Stronger than aspirin then.)** Kenneth seems unperturbed by the news, but I notice his list of questions remains in his pocket, unasked.

We drive to the cottage in virtual silence, our minds working overtime. How come I feel so well when the cancer is so widespread? Perhaps there's been a mix-up. Perhaps there's another Lynne Ives at the Cromwell who has lymphoma, and I'm in the clear.

I've never had any difficulty sleeping and I try to stay awake long enough to see the cancer in my mind's eye. I picture it as a large, grey, multi-headed dragon. I have six Knights – Brian Blessed, Oliver Reed, Bernard Manning, Keith Healy (a platonic pal of long standing), Malcolm and Kenneth. A motley crew for the most part, with the reputation of being beer-swilling, womanising chauvinists. I've never met Sir Brian or Sir Oliver and have only met Sir Bernard a few times, but I instinctively feel that all six would lay down their lives without hesitation for a damsel in distress. Sure enough they charge the dragon and have no trouble decapitating it, time after time. The problem is, as each head hits the ground it bursts into a thousand little crabs that go skittering off into the far reaches of my body. The dragon **looks** fearsome, but it's rooted to the spot and not very intelligent, so doesn't present much of a problem. The crabs, on the other hand, do. I'll have to change the mental image of the cancer.

There's dissension among the troops as I fall asleep. Sir Brian is loud-mouthing Sir Bernard, who is assaulting the other five with caustic wit; Sir Oliver has fallen off his mount (**pissed**), Sir Keith (**famed for sartorial elegance**) is annoyed about the dragon blood on his armour; Sir Kenneth has lost his specs and makes a quixotic charge in the wrong direction; and Sir Malcolm is miffed by all this disorderly conduct. Still, a fine job, lads! Thank you.

Sunday 16 October

I'm in Birmingham today, guesting on a special Christmas recording of 'Bullseye' for Central T.V.

I'm to play a dumb show hostess (**what d'you mean, 'play'?**), a 'surprise' Christmas present for Jim. I'm to stand in a huge foil-wrapped box, the sides of which collapse in a puff of smoke at the touch of a remote control button held by Jim. The box and pyrotechnics take a long time to set up, so we can't rehearse and have to hope it will be all right on the night. On the burst of tumultuous applause that will erupt at the mere sight of me, I am to wiggle my way forward, hug Jim and take over the show. Fine.

I'm wearing a black figure-hugging knee-length frock, which has been hand-embroidered all over with dangling jet beads; *sharp*, dangling jet beads that make standing up imperative. It's show time. I'm in the box sporting a new spiky hair-do, holding my stomach in and trying to remember what comes after 'Good evening' when the world explodes. I'm not prepared for the deafening 'bang' as the sides of the box collapse and my moment of entry is masked by puthers of 'smoke'. A muttering audience coughs and squints through the smoke to find out what the hell's going on, and only a mild smattering of, 'Oh, it's her' applause greets me as I stagger out of the smoke towards Jim. **(They were hoping for Tom O'Connor.)**

The show gathered momentum quickly and finished on a high that lasted through the party held afterwards at the neighbouring Holiday Inn. I'm not really a party-goer, so just popped my head in to bid my good nights, and hit the road home about 1 a.m. I have to be at Alyn Ainsworth's house tomorrow morning to sort keys for next week's appearance on 'Live from the Palladium'.

Tom Jones is topping the bill and among others, Joe Longthorne is guesting. I read somewhere that Joe has lymphoma. I wonder if I should talk to him about it? I've been taking chlorambucil for six days now and the lumps are diminishing with staggering rapidity. I have no side effects whatsoever. I seem to respond well to drugs. **(You didn't do too well on acid.)**

I was overjoyed when my Mom (and Blackie the cat) returned to Sheffield around 1955 and, with the help of my Pop, rented a small terraced house on the other side of Sheffield. I moved in with her immediately and changed schools (*again*), visiting my Pop at weekends. She seemed to have got her act together and held down a steady job as a capstan lathe operator in a local tool factory. She was really trying.

We got on together very well, our conversation frank and adult, with certain forbidden areas. Sex was one, my only instruction being, 'A man is like a woman, only inside out.' (*Still can't figure that one.*) And when my periods began I thought I had piles.

Money, of course, was scarce, and to help pay the bills she began to take in lodgers, moving me in to share her bedroom and letting my room and the attic. Most of the lodgers were transient steel erectors, working for short periods on small jobs and then moving on.

They were a mixed bunch, O.K. for the most part – one had to be thrown out for drawing genitals on Arthur the doll, thus adding to my scant sexual knowledge, and one, a regular called John, was particularly charming and handsome.

They fell head over heels in love and my real Mother returned, making a brief but dazzling comeback before crashing on to the spikes of despair once more when John fell to his death from a lofty scaffold, and history repeated itself.

The pills reappeared. She started drinking heavily, and fellow drunks would return with her from the pub on Friday nights. The party would continue into the wee small hours of oblivion, then pick up again on Saturday mornings when, after a breakfast of Anadin and hair-of-the-dog, they would return to the pub to begin again. She would return alone at 3.30 in the afternoon. If she wasn't home by then I'd have to go and fetch her, knowing she'd be slumped in a drunken stupor on the pavement, open-legged and snotty-nosed, against the wall of the High Fields pub. Sometimes I'd have to sit with her until she was sober enough to stand and I could shoulder her home, snapping a curt reply, 'It's all right, I can take care of her,' to kind enquirers.

The Friday night parties rarely affected me. Straight from school, I would catch a bus on my regular weekend pilgrimage to my Pop's house, an hour across the city. The contrast between my two guardians was vivid: Victorian discipline versus total freedom. Occasionally I'd find an excuse to stay with my Mom and would sneak down to watch the proceedings through any available spy-hole. After several complaints from neighbours, they were reasonably subdued affairs. Little groups of people drinking or sharing pungent hand-rolled cigarettes to the accompaniment of Radio Luxembourg.

On one occasion a small eye-dropper-type bottle was offered round and I watched, curious, as the few accepters tilted a drop of the contents on to an index finger and then rubbed the finger around their gums.

I would begin my much-loved cleaning the moment they all left for the pub, and in pursuit of domestic perfection removed the cushions from the couch to find the little brown eye-dropper-bottle. I unscrewed the cap and sniffed at a minute drop of liquid – it was odourless. I stood the bottle on the tiled mantel and continued my chores, rewarding myself with a coffee and a stolen Woodbine in front of the newly-made fire, before fetching the groceries from the corner shop.

The little brown bottle caught my eye again, and putting my cup and saucer down I uncapped and re-examined it. I tilted the bottle against my finger and sniffed again at the clear residue, wondering what to do, then (nothing ventured, nothing gained), rubbed my wet finger round my gums. Nothing.

I picked up my cup and saucer and flopped down on to the half-moon hearthrug, curious as to what the desired effect of the substance was supposed to be, and wondering why it hadn't worked, when I noticed the saucer felt thicker. How strange! I balanced the cup and saucer on the palm of one hand and watched as the saucer became thicker and thicker until it was a foot deep, then noticed the same thing happening to the half-moon rug. It was rising like a sponge cake. I lay down and gripped the edges as the rug bubbled and rose beneath me. Soon my buttocks were pressing against the ceiling, then the back of my head, and I hauled myself to the edge of the rug to look for a way down before I was crushed.

A skylight above the street door was closed and out of reach, but I tried to reach it anyway and was surprised when my fingers touched the ledge. I tried to get a better grip but to my horror my fingers began to run down the door like melting plasticine as I watched from my perilous vantage point. They raced to the bottom of the door at an alarming rate and then vanished, as if sucked, under the door, over the storm board, down the steps and across the pavement. I could feel the different textures of wood, gravel and asphalt racing beneath my fingers as they came to rest on the road, and was terrified of a car coming up the cul-de-sac and smashing my hand.

I felt something wet on my leg and turned round to see a coffee stain spreading across a now ordinary hearth-rug and my fingers once more where they should be. Thank God, it was over. I cleaned up the spill and walked down to the corner shop with my grocery list and three ten-bob notes to pay off last week's 'strap'.

Mr and Mrs Smith, the benign proprietors, were always good to me, giving me a lolly or a 'black jack' every time I shopped there, and I was looking forward to the treat as I stood behind a small queue masking the counter. As my turn approached and the queue thinned, I was afforded an occasional glimpse of the Smiths as they moved to collect purchases from the shelves behind them. Something strange had happened to them.

*They sounded the same and wore the same white overalls,
but Mr Smith had cloven hands – like a hoof with wiry brown
hair – sticking from the starched overall sleeves. Worse, emerg-
ing from the Dr Kildare collar was the head of a wild boar, complete with curly brown tusks. Mrs Smith was a wild boar too, yet
it was quite easy to differentiate them, as their expressions and
personalities remained the same and Mr Smith regarded me
kindly with little red eyes through the specs on the end of his
snout. I was fascinated by the droplets of saliva sticking to the
coarse stubby brown hair surrounding his mouth, and he had to
repeat his request for my shopping list.*

*The other customers retained their normal appearances and
didn't seem to notice anything odd about Mr and Mrs Smith, who
were still boars as I backed out of the shop carrying the bags of
groceries.*

*On discovering the bottle on the mantel where I'd left it, my
mother became quite agitated.*

'Where did you find this? You haven't taken any, have you?'

'No.'

'Thank God. It's L.S.D.'

It's been a frantic week of fittings and production meetings. The 'New Faces' gowns are almost ready; can't wait
to pick them up, it always gives me a special buzz driving through London with the back seat full of beautifully
made, exclusively designed gowns. Is this really happening or is it a wonderful dream? Nip. No, it's real.

John Peacock – friend and fellow Aquarian – is my
designer. He's a man of rare talent and is quite strong
with me. We spend 90 per cent of our design meetings
drinking coffee, gossiping and giggling. The remaining
10 per cent, I sit back and let John manipulate me.

'You're never a problem, Mart, you always know

exactly what you want . . .' and continues blowing hot air up my kilt until I end up with exactly what *he* wants. He's always right, of course, and I wouldn't dream of cluttering his designs with jewellery etc. without his approval.

The woman who makes my gowns wishes to remain anonymous, so I'll refer to her as 'M'. 'M' is more than a mere dressmaker, she's an artist: a fairy godmother sewing with enchanted thread, bringing, life to each John Peacock creation. Her gowns seduce me, sliding over me, caressing and squeezing, yards of whispering silk promising total femininity. They always fit perfectly, look painted on, and some have caused quite a furore in the past.

A ribbon-lace Verity Lewis creation once stopped the show and made the front page of the *Mirror* on its debut in a B.B.C. dance routine for the 1980 'Marti' series. Jeff Richer had choreographed the salacious routine, which began with me oozing down a cat-walk in a long black velvet evening coat and sliding it off my shoulders as I turn to camera revealing the lace gown. I looked naked under the lace (**the desired effect**), but in fact 'M' always makes built-in underwear out of fine flesh-coloured fabric with several linings of asbestos and a Liberty bodice under the lot for good measure.

Another 'front page' dress was an expensive mistake for the Royal Command Performance in 1979. It was a solid hand-beaded backless polo/halter-neck sheath, split to the hip on both sides. The back scooped down to 4 inches below my waist, but the weight of the beads stretched the base fabric and on the dress rehearsal, much to my embarrassment, the backless gown inched its way over my buttocks until it became not only backless but bottomless. The situation was saved by Sellotape, safety-pins and a few strategically placed orchids.

I'm playing the evil Red Queen in a play about Snow White over the Christmas Season. It's a wonderful part. I intend to do it in a proper English accent (**You can do it**). I tried it out on Kenneth, who talks like Prince Charles, and he was quite impressed. John Peacock has designed the gown, of course, and he took me to meet Martin Adams who is making the crown. Martin turned out to be a delightful man; I liked him instantly. His workshop is in Lotts Road, Chelsea and is an Aladdin's cave; trays of coloured gemstones, yards of sequins, buttons, beads, feathers and fans, gleaming armour, golden Egyptian mummies' masks and much more are crammed with ordered chaos into the small rooms housing several staff, all happily hammering, stitching and gluing.

I also had a meeting with the dress designer for the Palladium show. He wants me in a purple gown to match the set and shows me drawings of the dancers' outfits. It seems very strange deciding on the outfits before we know what routine we're doing. I know Alan Harding, the choreographer, well and a meeting in Nottingham earlier in the week has brought us no closer to a decision. We first danced together under Jeff Ritcher back in the seventies. He's a powerful dancer and, knowing him, the routine will be legs, lifts and back-bends. I have reservations about the gown, and the designer and I decide on purple trousers and a lilac shirt – that way I'm covered.

It's 3 a.m. when I get back to the cottage. I make a coffee and flick through a few albums to try and find something suitable – a Michael Sembelo, a Philip Baily, a

Deacon Blue, but none of them feel right in my soul. I miss my Sheffield flat; I have hundreds of albums up there.

4

Sunday 23 October

Some say they preferred Tom Jones before his nose job. Me? I never got as far as his nose. Nothing changes, I'm sitting in the stalls of the London Palladium gazing up at Tom Jones' loud American-checked crutch. He's raunching his way through his own version of 'Kiss', copulating with a flaccid mike wire and making Prince look like Pinocchio. An E minor when it should have been an E major brings the rehearsal to yet another halt while the suspect note is cordially argued over by the boys in the band. This gives wardrobe and make-up girls an opportunity to fluff round the star. Joe Longthorne pops his head round the proscenium arch on the way to his dressing room. I've decided to ask him about his lymphoma, perhaps after the tea-break.

My costume fits O.K.; the tight velvet pants worked well in the dance routine work-through this morning. On Monday I agreed to Alyn Ainsworth's suggestion of

Cole Porter's 'Smoke Gets In Your Eyes'. It's not the right song for the show, but we had so little time and a decision had to be made. I pre-recorded it to a click track on Tuesday – very nervously, it's been years since I sang – and will mime it with a live orchestra tonight. The rest of the week has been taken up with dance rehearsals which, thanks to my futile flailings, are usually hysterical.

Most of my 'showbiz' friends are dancers. I love working with them. They're a breed apart who work damned hard for little consideration. They literally bleed for a living. I walk into a dance rehearsal as a well-adjusted 44-year-old woman holding on to my valiums and the hope that I'm growing old gracefully, and I walk out a 19-year-old hooligan with purple hair extensions, leopard-skin cycling shorts, black lip-gloss and the word 'menopause' blocked out of my consciousness.

There is no earthly reason why I shouldn't be able to move like these young athletes. All those years at Sally Carmichael's dancing classes followed by weight training, then aerobics and, more recently, yoga, means I can still do high kicks and splits and back-bends with no trouble, but when I try to dance – I fall over. I trip and stumble, leaving crushed feet and kicked shins in my wake; I start on my left foot, they on their right; I move north when they move south. I'm hopeless. I lurch around taking spastic angular steps, like a crane about to topple. Jeff Ritcher, my choreographer, has spent most of the thirteen years he's worked on me with his head in his hands crying with laughter or frustration. Undaunted, I persevere.

Alan Harding, having worked with me on numerous occasions, knows my limitations and has allowed plenty of time. Even though I only have to walk around the dancers, he's taking no chances.

Kenneth is still poring over his books, looking for a cure, and is probably in the garden shed at this very moment, brewing rhubarb leaves and goat manure in an attempt to find one.

Tea-break is ten minutes away, so I slide through the pass door to check my costume before dress run. Tom Jones stands in the corridor like a James Bond poster – legs apart, arms folded, surrounded by pussy galore. I try not to stare and saunter past holding my breath. **(You can get pregnant sniffing his armpits!)**

'Hello, Marti,' and he steps forward and offers his hand **(that's all?)** God, he knows who I am.

'Hello, Tom,' I smile, shaking the proffered hand, and staying in his clasp too long for decency. Then hover, wondering whether to talk or not. Fate decides. The lovely Sinita glides by like a panther swathed in loin-cloth, boob tube and boots and takes his eyes with her. Thwarted, I walk on and barely have time to savour the moment before bumping into Joe.

Joe Longthorne is an abundantly talented performer and on first meeting him during the early days of his success I was struck by his lack of conceit. He was quiet and calm, listened politely to direction and readily complied.

This time he seemed ill at ease and jumpy and I noticed his face was slick with perspiration when he spun to greet me. He's in the dressing room next door and, after sorting himself out, he knocked and joined me in mine, giving me the opportunity to ask him about his illness. He paced around constantly drying his hands on a handkerchief, sat, then stood and paced some more. He explained that part of his treatment was a steroid which made him hyperactive and sweaty, and cursed the fact that he couldn't keep still. I asked what type of lymphoma he had. He said he didn't really know; it was all so bloody complicated, all he knew for sure was there were two types, aggressive and non-aggressive; one was curable and one wasn't and he – thank God – had the one that was. I told him that I had the one that wasn't – but had no symptoms at all and even felt 'high'.

He said to watch out for imagination. Each new ache or pain is not necessarily related to the illness. I'll remember that. I told him about my Knights – without revealing their identities – and he agreed that a lot can be achieved with the mind, that attitude is everything, and that life's 'hard knocks' shape your character. A summons from the tannoy interrupted our homespun philosophies and Joe sped off to perform a faultless run-through with no sign of the steroid-induced agitation – a true pro – while I sat and thought about life's 'hard knocks'.

A long relationship with the local police began two weeks after my Mother's marriage to George Fisher (no Cinderella story is complete without a wicked step-parent.) He was a fellow Scot and alcoholic and the union was born more out of desperation than love. I could understand the attraction. He had a dangerous, Richard Burton quality about him and, when sober, he was funny, warm and generous. But whisky turned him into a savage bully. In fairness, most of his anger was incurred by my Mother's drug-taking habit, which she was unable to give up.

One night, alarmed by her screams, I ran downstairs to find the lounge in disarray and my Mother pinned to the floor with a bloodied face and bulging eyes, straddled by George who had his hands around her throat.

I leapt on to his back, fists flying, and sank my teeth into his shoulder, drawing blood. In an attempt to shake me off, his elbow smashed into my face, breaking my nose and a canine tooth.

These violent rituals became a regular event and the police and I were soon on first-name terms, although most of the beatings took place at the week-ends when I was at my Pop's house. I copped for mine mid-week, always in defence of my Mother. Eventually I realised that a weapon could be more effective than my 11-year-old fists and depleted teeth, so I smashed an empty milk bottle over his head. I thought I'd killed him, but my dread was replaced by fear as he began to come round. Deciding that attack was the best form of defence, I knelt beside him and lowering my head to within inches of his, said, 'Next time, It'll be the bread knife.'

He believed me and the next day suggested that I moved out.

I moved back in with my Grandfather, changing schools once again and seeing my Mom at week-ends.

I adored my Pop, and loved playing the role of 'little mother', cleaning, washing and darning his socks. On the day I moved in my Mother had warned me not to let him rule my life like he'd ruled my Father's, but it never occurred to me to disobey him and seemed natural to follow the 'week planner' he'd written out and pinned to the notice-board in the kitchen:

Monday	– Washing
Tuesday	– Ironing
Wednesday	– Youth Club etc.

With blind obedience, I allowed him to organise my life until the age of 12, when I underwent a sudden and dramatic personality change.

When she was good
She was very very good.
But when she was bad
She was wicked.

The cause was a common one and as old as the hills, but I was unable to talk about it for years. It was nothing really, nothing at all, yet it devastated me and affected me more profoundly than any previous or subsequent event.

I found him in bed with me.

There was a thunderstorm and I struggled from a deep sleep. What was happening? I was holding something. It felt like my wrist, but couldn't have been, and as I reached the surface of consciousness, it was jerked from my hand and I was rocked fully awake by suddenly unburdened bedsprings as my Pop leapt from my bed to stand beside me.

'You were having a nightmare, chick,' he said and his face looked gaunt and anguished in the spill from the street-lamp as he rearranged the bedclothes, making a 'little nest' for me before he left the room, pulling his nightshirt round him.

In a blinding flash, everything fell into place. The previous year, when my lifestyle was reversed and I was living with my Mom mid-week, I'd bring my pal Sally to stay for the week-end at Pop's. Sal was a couple of years older than me and Pop would spoil us rotten – meals on trays in front of the telly, day trips to Belle Vue fun park or Blackpool – so I was surprised when one week she refused the usual invitation. When I asked why, she tried to tell me as gently as she could, but I didn't understand – 'Your Pop comes into our room at night.' So what? Probably just checking to see we were O.K. Now it all made sense and I thought back to all the others who had suddenly stopped visiting: Cathy, Victoria, Jean.

It was a new me who demanded locks on my bedroom door

the next day. The incident was never mentioned. I felt ashamed and kept the secret, not even sharing it with Pam until we were in our twenties. But I began to rebel and he was fully aware why. If Pop said, 'Don't', I did; if he said 'black', I said 'white' and I punished him daily, one way or another. What he did was relatively harmless, yet somewhere deep down it damaged me and gave me a streak of recklessness that is still having consequences even today.

He reacted to my mute accusations by growing sullen and brooding. While life continued normally on the surface, it was never the same. He became more puritanical, searching my room and handbag regularly. He wouldn't allow me to wear stockings, and I was still in knee-socks and lace-ups when I left school. Brassieres were unmentionable and my dark aureoles and prominent nipples would show through my school blouse and vest. To avoid embarrassment I'd stick plasters over them to keep them down. 'Sanitary towel' were dirty words, and I would steal two shillings from his pocket to buy them when the need arose.

I continued to punish him, even when I wasn't with him. I kept a set of clothes at my Mother's house – she treated me as a contemporary, so allowed me to do as I wished – and on Friday afternoons, I'd catch the bus from school to spend the week-end there. On Friday nights, between the ages of 13 and 15, I would go dancing – the 'Over Twenty-One Night' at the Locarno.

I'd swap my vest and plasters for a Marks and Spencer circle-stitched bra, a rigid, pointed contraption that made me look as if I had a couple of ice-cream cones up my jumper: I could never fill them to the end (not even on a good day) and the last waltz would result in dents in the ends. I would change my school knickers, knee-socks and lace-ups for stockings, suspenders and high heels. Stockings were never long enough and the tension between suspender and stocking-top would result in spring-loaded legs; if you had to run for a bus, the legs would *keep going for three stops. My grey school skirt would be swapped for a rock-and-roll dirndl and six net petticoats, painstakingly dipped in sugar water to make them stiff when dry; after the first four dances, the heat from my body would melt the sugar and my nylons would stick together. I'd stand for hours in front of the mirror, painting my face and fingernails and backcombing and lacquering from a sticky, plastic squeeze bottle until my hair resembled a busby. Had my Pop passed me in the street, he wouldn't have recognised me.*

On Friday nights, I'd stay out till Saturday and my friends envied me and would say, 'I wish my mother was more like yours,' and I'd think, 'I wish mine was more like yours.'

My life seemed a mess. I couldn't wait to grow up, defying Pop at every opportunity. On my sixteenth birthday I walked into the house with a fag in every orifice; I was legally old enough to smoke, so, I thought, just try and stop me! He did try and the punishment continued. Perhaps I'm still punishing him by penning this recollection, or am I perhaps finally laying the ghost?

The tannoy interrupts again, pulling me out of my reverie and making my heart pound; it's my call. The fear never lessens.

Jimmy Tarbuck is rabbiting on in front of the tabs, the dancers are in position, stretching their limbs and adjusting their costumes, bathed in the blue of first lighting condition. I stand, hands cold, nose running, breath coming hard, I'm on. I'm off. It's over.

5

I'm expecting the boys for dinner tomorrow and looking forward to it. It's rare to get them both together. I've managed not to ruin the beef casserole and defrosted what I think is a plum crumble – circa January 1986. I arrived last night after a thought-filled journey, rehearsing the words, changing the dialogue, trying to find some sort of padding to soften the blow. (**Don't think about it, I'll handle it.**) I decide to stop thinking about it and just let it happen.

Lee opened the door away from my poised key. He was about to shower and, in the white towel he was wearing, allayed any subconscious maternal fear that he wasn't eating properly.

'Who are you?' I demanded. Ignoring me he kissed my cheek – 'Hiya, Ma!' – and I followed my Commando son to two waiting mugs and a boiling kettle in the kitchen. We exchanged small talk while he made coffee; what were his plans?

'Immediate or long-term?'

'Immediate.'

He was meeting the lads at seven and I wasn't to wait up as he might not be home till February (a chip off the old block). O.K., if I insisted he would stay for dinner with Max tomorrow evening, and could I let him know what I was planning to cook as he would like to start working on the antidote.

Dodging the hurled dishcloth he slipped through the door, leaving me to sip my coffee and breathe in the sweet smells of home. The place is in the same gleaming order as when I left it last, the only sign of Lee's presence being the neatly made camp-bed and a regimented row of balled socks beside his kit-bag in the dining room.

He's always been tidy. As a kid, his room was kept in strict order, books and toys respected and playthings returned to private cupboards, hidden away like his emotions. He was born independent, self-sufficient and still is, and I'm left to wonder where the time went.

Malc and I were all part of the same gang when we were 14, sort of 'paired off' when we were 15, and started putting our biology theory into practice at 16.

We were both still 16 when the doctor confirmed I was pregnant. (It was after the Cricket Lover's Ball.) When I told Malc, he turned up the next night with a gift-wrapped teddy for the baby. Telling my Pop was going to be the worst bit. He didn't smoke, didn't drink and, as far as I knew, hadn't put his biology theory into practice since my Grandmother's death in 1953.

Despite our differences, Pop had big dreams for me. He con-

centrated on training me to become an Olympic athlete. Every evening I'd return from school, do my chores and my homework (and smoke five Woodbines), then meet him at Corporation Street baths at 5.30. For two hours he'd have me swimming after a brush held in front of my nose, while he set the pace up and down the side of the baths. This is where my acting career began – I developed the most spectacular cramps, flailing about in the water, gasping, coughing and protesting, 'Don't worry, Pop, just give me a moment and I'll be fine . . . cough!'

Four days later found me out in the garden learning the 'Western roll' over a beautifully (if hastily) made high-jump frame. He was tenacious, that man! He was also possessive; he only allowed me out twice a week – Wednesday's Youth Club and Thursday's Sally Carmichael's dancing class – and accompanied me to both (pity he didn't come to the Cricket Lover's Ball).

It was while I was attending Sally Carmichael's dancing class that I accidentally entered a beauty contest – the local Working Men's Club where we practised was running a 'Queen of Sheffield Working Men's Clubs' contest. The committee, in their own inimitable style, had eliminated too many girls and were left with only four for the final. In desperation, they asked Sally Carmichael for eight of her tallest girls to make up the line. The fact that I was only 14 and under age by four years (and covered in bruises from playing football with the lads) didn't matter. I was 5ft 8in, 36-22-36 and with a new perm and a borrowed swimsuit and high heels, I won.

That was it! Pop had a new ambition. I was going to be a model. The high-jump stand was thrown into the garage and I entered the Grove Model School on a 20-week course. By the time I was 16, I was winning major contests, amassing a few quid in the bank as a part-time model and walking as though I had a brush handle up my arse. My Grandfather accompanied me to all contests and modelling assignments and was well known on the Beauty Queen circuit as 'Pop'. 1962 was to be my big year; Pop had me weight training three times a week, my statistics were now 40-24-36 and I was in the final of the Mecca 'Miss England' Contest. The news of my pregnancy would shatter him (convincing him of an immaculate conception would have been easier.)

I decided to try and find my Mother.

Her marriage had continued to slide downhill until eventually, after being evicted from the house, she divorced my stepfather for persistent cruelty, and took a job as the live-in caretaker of a seedy block of flats.

Thanks to her 'habits' the job didn't last long, and she moved away from Sheffield in 1960, sending a note to say she'd keep in touch.

I finally found her in Chester. She was doing all right as a nursing orderly in a geriatric hospital – one of her favourite 'legitimate' jobs as it gave her easy access to sleeping pills and downers.

'If it's a boy – call him William,' was her response to the news. We were wandering round the Zoo at the time, and a small boy dropped his ice-cream cone down my Courreges boot. Reading my thoughts, she continued, 'Don't have it adopted. That kid you wanted to strangle just now might have been yours and you wouldn't have known.'

'What if Pop throws me out?'

'You'll cope, Lynne – you can cope with anything. Lend us a quid?'

Malc and I decided we'd have to face the music and tell his parents and my Pop. He was working for his cousin in Sheffield market as an apprentice butcher, but had bought a trumpet and intended, one day, to become Louis Armstrong.

His cousin knew of our predicament and had informed

Malc's parents before we had a chance to break the news ourselves. They were terrific – upset, but very sympathetic and his
Mother said not to worry, if Pop threw me out she'd look after
me. We all took the short bus-ride to my Pop's house.

I ran ahead. I had to tell him the news myself.

'Hello Pop, Mr and Mrs Stringer are here to see you.'

'Oh?'

'Yes, I'm pregnant.' (What sweet revenge.)

He fell into the chair as though he'd been hit with a medi-
cine ball and said very little while Malc's parents discussed what
we should do. They decided that he'd have to marry me. At this,
Pop came to life and leapt from his chair.

'Don't get married, you don't have to. Don't get married!
You can go to your Uncle Frank's in Blackpool, then we can
have it adopted, no one will know. Don't get married.'

I thought back to the kid with the ice-cream in Chester Zoo.

'I don't want to have it adopted, I want to keep it.'

'Don't be ridiculous. You're sixteen. You're only a kid yourself.'

My Scots chin shot out and, spotting the familiar defiance in
my eyes, he changed his tune. 'O.K., O.K., you can keep it, but
DON'T GET MARRIED.'

We got married. Malc sold his trumpet to buy me a wedding
ring. A wedding was arranged at St Christopher's Church.
Malc's large, happy family filled a quarter of the church, Pop
and my Mom filled a quarter of a pew and the rest of the church
was bursting at the seams with most of the council estate,
curious as to whether I was 'showing' or not.

I walked down the aisle, sobbing uncontrollably, in a cream
Wallis suit with hand-made replacement buttons costing more
than the suit. (Silly tart.) Malc was kneeling at the altar and a
price ticket of 39/11d (nearly two quid) decorated the sole of his
shoe. (More expensive than a marriage licence, but they'll

probably last longer.)

Malc's Mom held a small reception for us, doing the catering herself (potted meat sandwiches with the crusts cut off) and paid for a four-day honeymoon in Blackpool, where the landlady would sell us contraceptives – I wasn't showing, and pride forced us to put on an act – but said we were too young to smoke and refused us cigarettes.

We returned from our honeymoon to live with my Pop. We found Sheffield strewn with uprooted trees and fallen chimneys, the result of a ferocious storm which began on our wedding day. Perhaps an omen of things to come.

Ralph Lauren's Polo aftershave came galloping into the kitchen, followed shortly by a now fully clothed Lee. He just had time for a quick coffee (it was now or never), and in the time I took to refill the kettle and put coffee into two clean mugs, I'd told him. I was matter-of-fact, and filled the statement with medical data and statistics, adding an assurance that I intended to beat the bastard. He reacted exactly as I had expected:

'Course you'll beat it, love – hope you're insured. By the way, you need some hundred-watt light bulbs. I'm off. See you later, Ma!'

Kiss, and he was gone, storing the information in his private cupboards, his face revealing nothing.

Max, at 6ft 3in, is an inch shorter than Lee, younger by twenty months and considered by outsiders to be the 'hunk' of the family. He has inherited his Father's good looks and his Grandmother's good nature and easygoing outlook, which is usually too easygoing for his Father's liking. He has a soft dark brown voice, which I have never heard him raise, an acute sense of the ridiculous, and we're extremely bad for each other. We share a Peter

Pan mentality, a lack of self-discipline and a strong streak of slob – which renders any room inhabited by the two of us into a bomb-site within minutes. We're both Aquarian dreamers and have always been able to be 'alone' together, or step easily into imagination games, and Max – like me – has a fairy godmother who always seems to save his neck at the last minute.

Max joined me for the last nine of my eighteen-months' stint in Sun City. On his eighteenth birthday he was allowed into the casino and, with a hundred Rand stake, won a thousand. The next night he lost it. On his walk back home, pockets empty, eyes downcast, he found a diamond bracelet with a reward value of two hundred Rand which won him another thousand.

This week, he was relief-managing a pub in Rotherham and I'd arranged to drive over to see him after 11 p.m. I arrived early and he led me upstairs to a comfortable polish-scented lounge and made coffee, before returning to the bar to finish off. It was near midnight by the time he rejoined me. He was terribly upset by my news. We talked until 4 a.m., finishing with a promise to meet this evening – despite the threatened meal.

My lack of culinary expertise has always been a source of great mirth to the men in my life and my well-attended failures embroidered into legends over the years, so I was prepared for the banter that accompanied dinner.

Lee – 'Something smells good – who cooked it?' I serve the meal. They sit in silence, hands in laps, eyeing the food suspiciously – a well-practised act.

Max – 'Er! What is it, please?'

'It's beef casserole, braised root vegetables, sprouts, Yorkshire pudding and creamed potatoes,' I reply, slipping into my part.

'Sounds delicious . . .' enthuses Max. 'Can I have a tuna sandwich?'

'Something moved!' says Lee, jerking away from the table and pointing in horror at Max's plate.

'It's O.K.,' says Max, gingerly lifting the edge of the Yorkshire pudding and peering beneath. 'It was just the gravy clotting.'

'Are you sure? Her gravy doesn't usually move,' and so on until the meal was over. They were supposedly going out to hit the high spots together, leaving me to throw some things into a bag and drive down to the cottage. Instead they stayed talking until the small hours, telling me of the strokes they'd pulled and the mischief they'd got into as kids – right under my unsuspecting nose!

Sunday 30 October

It was 5 a.m. when I hit the M1 after leaving Lee at the flat and dropping Max off at his pub, and was quite tired when I reached the cottage at around 7.30 this morning. Common sense tells me I should get more sleep, as my work-load is quite heavy at the moment. (**What the hell – live every second of life.**) Last week was another frantic cocktail of fittings, production meetings, voice-overs and charities, topped by a long photographic session and interviews for *T V Times*. Still, I'm glad I stole Friday and Saturday to see the boys, and after a couple of hours' sleep, I awoke refreshed and looking forward to the arrival of David Grindrod for lunch.

David must be the best company manager in the

business, and our friendship goes back a decade or more. Kenneth adores him and commandeered him the moment he arrived, allowing me to join them on a walk after yet another edible meal (**any more of this clever cooking and you'll ruin your reputation**). The cottage is set on the highest ridge of the Chiltern Hills and is surrounded by the most glorious countryside. Kenneth came across it while returning from a far-flung artist's studio where he'd been to purchase a John Miller watercolour for my birthday. We'd been living in his London flat, and so far our frantic house-hunt had been futile – too big, too small, too near the road, too far from London, but mostly too expensive. This one was just about right, though it bulged our financial boundaries, and we moved in with the previous owners' carpets and curtains and little else. I intend to start alterations in spring and am determined not to be thwarted by cancer (**far less, the mere lack of money**). As for the money – it will fall from the sky.

We returned from our walk aglow with wind-reddened cheeks, divested ourselves of boots and outer layers of wrapping and flopped down in the deep chairs of the sunset-lit lounge chatting, until David left at around 10 p.m.

Lovely day, early night.

Friday 1 November

It's dark, cold and pouring with rain as I leave the office of E. and B. Productions where I've been discussing the pantomime orchestra with Paul, the company musical director. Not only is it raining, it's 5 o'clock, and though

I'm not defeatist by nature I don't even bother looking for a taxi, deciding instead to walk the two miles back to the London flat. Though my head is uncovered, I'm wearing a huge black rubber raincoat – my favourite – and slinging my holdall over my shoulder, tuck my cold blue hands into the wide warm sleeves and strike out towards home.

I squelch upstairs to the flat after my half-hour walk, and Kenneth answers the door with his specs on the end of his nose and the now permanent book in his hand. He stands in the doorway, forcing me to continue dripping in the hall, and says:

'Hello. Listen to this: 'Large cell centroblastic/centrocytic type lymphoma is a B-cell malignancy composed of. . . .'

I gently pushed him aside and walked in and he followed me around reading with great enthusiasm while I poured the contents of my shoes down the sink, removed my coat and made us both a hot drink, interjecting now and again with, 'Fancy that!' 'Really?' and. 'Ger' away!'

Over the past few weeks, Kenneth's every waking moment has been spent poring over his medical books, phoning oncologists, pathologists and an assortment of scientists, asking for explanations and information on the subject of malignant lymphoma. He has become an expert layman (**and a doctor groupie**). He's read papers on the subject, visited laboratories and driven me mad reading out passages that sound like a foreign language. Oddly enough these men of science are not only willing but *eager* to talk on their subject, and to that end he's invited the author of his present reading matter to lunch on Sunday to explain about '. . . anti-idiotypic monoclonal antibodies, that . . .'

Visitors for lunch on Sunday. I don't think I'll push my present run of culinary luck any further; I'll go to M. & S. tomorrow and buy something ready-made. It's been the usual frantic week, beginning with a local press and radio call in Cambridge for the panto. The high spot of the week was having lunch with Ronnie Hazlehurst, musical director for the B.B.C., fellow-Northerner and pal of long standing. We never run out of conversation, although it knocked the wind out of his sails when I told him the news and he suggested I contact a faith-healer friend of his.

I'm driven to an early night by Kenneth's reading. I put my Knights to work and drift into sleep.

6

Sunday 6 November

I knew I shouldn't have pushed my culinary luck. John Habeshaw, Ph.D., M.D., one of the British scientists working on the AIDS virus and one of the country's leading authorities on malignant lymphoma, was throwing up in the cloakroom. Instinct told me it was going to be one of those days the moment I removed the little grey shrivelled chicken from the oven. A pre-warned Kenneth had plied John and his girl-friend Rosie with champagne to deaden the effect of the coming lunch, as I chased huge lumps round a pan of watery pulp that started life as potato.

The ploy worked. Rosie is a tall, slim attractive woman, an interior designer with Laura Ashley, and seems cool, calm and collected – we clicked at once. John is the modern-day version of an absent-minded boffin: hair unruly, specs askew, collar curling away from a foreign tie and odd socks. He and Kenneth started con-

'I was naughty sometimes. I once took all eleven of my dad's Angel Fish to school in a jam jar and poured them into the pond to keep the goldfish company.'

'My parents were always in each other's arms. Our home was full of laughter and love, Dick Barton... crisp sheets, and shiny furniture.'

'Despite our differences, Pop had big dreams for me. On Wednesdays Pop took me to Sally Carmichael's Dancing Class…'

'If Pop said don't, I did; if he said black, I said white and I punished him daily, one way or another. What he did was relatively harmless, yet it damaged me and was the cause of reckless behaviour with consequences as far reaching as now.' (photo: *Sheffield Star and Telegraph*)

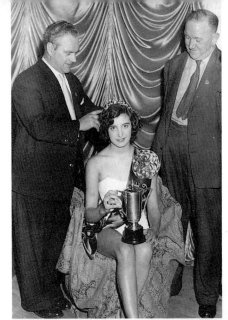

'I was only fourteen and under age by four years (and covered in bruises from playing football with the lads). I was 5 ft 8 inches, 36-22-36, with a new perm and a borrowed swimsuit and high heels; to a blind man on a galloping horse I looked like a professional beauty queen. I won.'

'I walked down the aisle in a cream Wallis suit... Malc was kneeling at the altar and a price ticket of 39/11 decorated the sole of his shoe.'

'... I caught sight of myself in the peeling mirror: long thin legs, blue from the cold, clashing with the bright pink mini-dress which began at my neck and finished at my knicker legs... I looked like a rag doll. They were expecting Princess Voluptua.'

'Malc is my ex-husband, we were married when we were seventeen and after eighteen years were divorced to a chorus of "I knew it wouldn't last!"'

versing using no fewer than five-syllable words before he'd even got out of the car, and have been rabbiting happily like two philatelists over a rare collection.

Put simply, John was almost convinced that most cancers are viruses; the immune system knows that the body has been invaded and sends out its army of anti-bodies who fail to recognise the enemy and so cannot destroy it. Before moving into AIDS research, John was one of a British team working on mouse antibodies that *did* recognise the enemy – or at least my particular enemy, low-grade follicular lymphoma. The mouse anti-body is matched and cloned with the patient's antibody and reintroduced into the patient, and is now able to recognise and destroy the cancer cells. They're called anti-idiotypic monoclonal antibodies and the work is being continued at Stanford University in California. It's still in the experimental stage, but they are accepting guinea-pigs if they have this particular strain of lym-phoma and, therefore, nothing to lose.

John finished by saying that if we wanted to know more about the Stanford University project, or needed an introduction, Professor Karol Sikora, head of oncology at Hammersmith Hospital, had worked there for eighteen months. This was wonderful news. Karol Sikora is head of the department in which Chris McKenzie, my own oncologist, works. I'm seeing Dr McKenzie tomorrow so perhaps he can arrange a meeting. Before retiring a de-cision is made: we're going to Stanford.

Monday 7 November

Encapsulated in their nose-to-tail cars, stranded drivers

read papers, picked their noses and talked to themselves, resigned to the rush-hour wait along the Chiswick High Road. I was already forty-five minutes late for a dental appointment and had plenty of time to reflect upon the day.

I had a successful 2 o'clock meeting with the organisers of a charity event to raise money for Guy's Hospital cancer unit. It's in conjunction with the London College of Fashion, and including all the up-and-coming young designers along with Miyake, Conran, Alaia etc., strutting their stuff to an invited audience. Each named designer is donating an outfit to be auctioned off and I'm the auctioneer.

Seventeen days have passed since I finished the ten day course of chlorambucil. The lumps on my body disappeared within days, but already I can feel the familiar 'bruising' sensations on my neck, an indication that one is about to appear. I mentioned it to Dr McKenzie this morning, adding that I nonetheless feel perfectly well. His strong, demanding fingers interrogated the lymph glands in my neck and armpits while Kenneth, now able to converse with authority on the subject, told him about John Habeshaw's visit and our newly-arrived-at decision to visit Stanford University. Before Kenneth had a chance to mention Professor Sikora, Dr McKenzie lifted the phone.

'Hello, Karol? . . . Chris. I have with me a Mrs Ives . . .' (The *Mrs Ives, if you don't mind!*) '. . . yes, I discussed her case with you some time ago. Mrs Ives and her husband are most interested in monoclonal antibodies and would, I feel, benefit from your wisdom.' Cupping the phone: 'Would tomorrow at 10 suit?' We nodded, pleased.

'Karol Sikora, my head of department, worked at Stanford on the very project you're describing. He'll be delighted to answer your questions.' He turned to me. 'Meanwhile, I think you should consider a bone-marrow harvest, in case we decide on a transplant at some future date.' And he fixed an appointment with Dr Wardle of Harley Street on Wednesday.

Apparently you have a pint of bone marrow removed – two doctors working together on opposite sides of the pelvic girdle suck the marrow through thin steel tubes – you don't feel a thing, it's all done under general anaesthetic and you wake up in your bed feeling a little bruised. That's all.

So far, so good.

The marrow is then frozen for up to ten years, or until the patient needs it. When all other methods have failed, the patient is blasted with radiation and chemotherapy so caustic that 10 per cent die. The survivor's bone marrow is by now reduced to ashes and the pre-harvested marrow is reinjected into the pelvis. The marrow regenerates itself rapidly while the patient spends the next three months in a plastic bubble; 30 per cent can expect total remission. When I saw Dr Wardle he booked me into the Princess Grace Hospital the following Wednesday. I have the bone-marrow harvest on Thursday.

Doubting whether the traffic jam would have cleared by Wednesday, I finally arrived in time to miss my dental appointment and searched my mind for something pleasant to think of as I rejoined the traffic and inched my way back to the cottage. My cassettes had been removed from the rack separating the front seats during a half-hearted attempt at car valeting, and I hadn't replaced them. Sticky tendrils of rain slithered down the semi-steamed windows of the idling Rolls, encouraging a creeping melancholia. A police car streaked by on the relatively traffic-free side of the M4, its siren's wail mournful, and the flashing light replaced the sodium yellow filling the car taking my mind to another time.

The night was slashed with alternate blue and then white light, and the street hung in that eerie awesome silence which accompanies the sudden stop of alarm bells. The ambulance doors closed out the white face of my recently acquired 17-year-old husband. The nurse at my side begged with a vomit bowl, and I donated with gusto, body trembling violently, teeth tight clenched to stop them chattering. I was in labour, and frightened. (Stay calm, stay calm, control it!)

The fear was abating, the trembling beginning to stop, a contraction chuckled in a place outside my body and began to pour molten lead uphill. A slow savage explosion of pain hit the places where months earlier, pleasure had hit, (the finer the pleasure, the finer the pain).

The Jessop Hospital for Women sucked me in and I was tucked into a dimmed ward containing three others – two delivered, one about to, by the sound of things. The ward was suddenly full of Attila the Hun in a nursing sister's uniform:

'Shut up, Mrs Robinson, you're only two fingers dilated. Mrs Stringer?' and the light above my bed snapped on. 'Good God! You're only a kid yourself, freckles, plaits and tits. Let's have a look at you, girlie!' and surprisingly gentle and capable hands enquired and soothed to the sounds of Mrs Robinson. Another contraction.

'Relax now, sweetheart, concentrate on breathing and count – there, yes – that's at its peak now, isn't it? Good girl. Good girl.' Her voice was soft and encouraging, I felt safe.

A wail from Mrs Robinson.

'Don't let that silly cow put you off, love, just remember to relax your stomach muscles and concentrate on counting. I'm knocking off now. I'll be back tonight – you'll still be here' – raising her voice slightly – 'and so will you, Mrs Robinson, so shut up!' She left.

Day shift came and went, the newly delivered mums returned home, and Mrs Robinson had a girl and ' . . . God knows 'ow many bleedin' stitches'. Sister Attila returned, winked, examined, congratulated and left. Malc came to visit. I was drenched in sweat, bottom sheet twisted in sinewy hands, but thanks to Sister Attila, I could control it. I was even quite enjoying it. The day had streaked by in a blur of concentration and counting. My enthusiasm transmitted itself to Malc and he left at the end of visiting time a happier man.

At 1 a.m. Attila wheeled me into her lair where at 2.20 a.m. I gave easy birth to an 8lb son. Attila purred and cooed, placed my naked son upon my breast and went out to make, 'A nice cup of hot, sweet tea!'

Where was it? Where was the wave of all-consuming love I was supposed to feel?

What was love anyway? Was it what I felt for Malc? I certainly felt lust and jealousy, but if that's all love was, it wasn't enough. Did Malc love me? (He thought he did, you knew he didn't.) We were the same age, but I was so much older than he. His life had been an annual week in Bridlington with liver on Tuesdays; a 'selection box' from Auntie Eve and a new two-wheeler one Christmas; washing airing round a coal fire on wet Mondays; Vick on his chest and wool vests in winter; 'Puddin's on't table, lads!' at 5.30 come hell or high water. Father calls her Mother, Mother calls him Father; always love; always warmth; always there.

He had never experienced loss or loneliness or real fear. He had never seen his parents as anything other than Mum and

Dad. I'd seen the naked soul of my Mother. I'd wiped her snotty nose and covered her lewd, spreadeagled indecency. I'd cleaned the spurious wounds and known humiliation, shame and hopelessness and for those very reasons, loved her the more.

I looked down at the perfect rosebud lips, the determined chin and the tiny clenched fists of my cub. He lay awake, still and quiet. Not for him the blind search for a nipple, no 'free of the womb' spasms to jerk his limbs; he was happy to be apart, independent, an entity unto himself.

What if this lack of maternal feeling meant I wasn't good enough for him? What if I wasn't capable of loving?

The thought worried me until about the sixth month of my second pregnancy. I was returning from shopping with 17-month-old Lee in his push-chair when a large brown dog attacked, snarling at the feet of my terrified infant. I'm afraid of dogs, but a rage the like of which I'd never known before – and rarely since – took hold of me and I wanted to kill it, rip it limb from limb and tear at its throat with my teeth. Parking the pram I gave chase to the poor beast who, alarmed by my savage roar of maternal fury, had bolted. Doing a Daley Thompson over hedges and shrubberies, rose-beds, ornamental pools and cold-frames. I pursued the howling dog, hands clawed and teeth bared, stopping only when my rage was replaced by the realisation that for the first time in my life I'd put another human being before myself.

I was stricken with a love so vast that I couldn't find the edges. It was without end or beginning, paling all emotional experiences into insignificance. I was shaken by its totality, its danger – here was a being that I knew I would die for without hesitation.

My enthusiasm had waned by the time the tea arrived. It was as if my life was over, my moment passed. I would be one of the Green Shield Stamp queue at Tesco. I'd join the crimplene brigade, dress out of the Littlewoods club and resign myself to false teeth and a perm by the time I was 30. I would learn to scream, 'Come 'ere, ya little bleeders!' at an 'Ovaltinie' line-up of offspring, and have a council house with 'Cardinaled' steps, net curtains and a telly on the never-never from Wigfalls. The highlights of my week would be bingo and Tupperware parties. (Boy! When you wane you really wane, don't you?)

It was day three when I started to haemorrhage and Lee cried for the first time since his brief squawk at the moment of birth. The girls used to tease me: 'Lynne, your baby's crying!' I'd belt back to the ward to find a peacefully sleeping child. Come to think of it, I never lost a night's sleep with either of my kids. They were so easy to raise. God must have sent good kids on the premise that my maternal inadequacies would ensure their return within the fortnight, had he sent anything too difficult.

They tried all day to stem the bleeding but failed, so decided to do an emergency op. I was too young to sign the consent form and when Malc arrived, he also was found to be too young. My Grandfather arrived and was found to be not my 'official' guardian, but despite red tape they finally carted me off to be cauterized.

All went well, Lee stopped crying, I stopped bleeding and my Mother walked in. I hadn't seen her since my wedding day, but had heard she was 'housekeeping' for some Pakistani gentlemen in Rotherham. My heart-rate increased automatically – trouble followed my mother around. She smiled at me, bent and kissed me. She smelled of booze and I adored her. She was beautiful – painfully thin, but beautiful, even with the ravages of drug abuse drawing her face. Love and pride shone from her enormous black eyes as, ever tender, she lifted her grandson and held him against her grubby sweater for a long moment before returning him to his crib.

'I've made him these.' Her nails black, her fingers blistered and nicotine-stained, she handed me a brown paper-bag. Inside were two tiny angel-top suits, white Viyella, beautifully made, with intricate pale blue smocking running across the yokes. 'You can't buy anything to actually fit a new-born baby.' She left. The garments fitted perfectly; he'd grown out of them in 3 weeks.

We were always so skint. We were sharing a two-bedroomed council house with my Pop, and although we only paid thirty bob towards the rent, we had two kids and Malc was earning just £4.10.0 a week as a butcher. (This was in the days when four pounds and ten shillings was worth sod all.)

I tried many ways of earning a few extra bob. I worked part-time as a waitress and office cleaner; I delivered plastic flower arrangements to pubs; I sharpened knives in a cutlery factory; worked lunch-times in a chip shop; delivered leaflets; demonstrated kitchen gadgets, to name but a few.

Having inherited my Mother's artistic streak and my Grandfather's practical one, I was always good at decorating and sewing. I made most of the kids' gear, all my own, most of Malc's trousers, and started taking in sewing for club-turns. Tom Jones had hit the scene wearing black horseshoe-necked, flared-leg catsuits – I must have made two dozen crimplene copies. I also tried my hand at professional decorating. I placed an advert in the post office window:

PROFESSIONAL DECORATING

WHOLE ROOMS – EMULSION	— £2.00
WHOLE ROOMS – WALLPAPER	— £3.00
CEILINGS	— £1.00

O.A.P.s – 20% DISCOUNT

I had my first client within days, an old lady who wanted her ceiling painted and the walls papered. I paid the woman next door a quid to look after Lee and Max, bought a roller and tray and a paste brush – another quid – borrowed a paste board, and at 8 a.m. skipped off to my first commission. Two a.m. the next morning found me dragging my aching body and borrowed paste board back towards home, having just stuck the last piece in place. Malc was furious, especially when I admitted that I hadn't the heart to charge the old dear, so we were two quid out of pocket.

Seduced by better money, Malc became a bus conductor and the bad times began. He was working with other 19-year-olds who didn't have a wife and two kids to support, and Malc wasn't mature enough to resist the lure of booze and birds. We saw less and less of each other and fought like tigers when we did spend time together. My Pop hated Malc from day one and the feeling was mutual. One particular fight left me sobbing long after Malc had stormed off to work. My Pop came to me with an old Army pistol in his hand, knelt beside me and said, 'If you want me to kill him, I will. They can't hang me. I'm too old.' I realised it was time to move out.

We tried living with Malc's parents and that was fine for a while. I adored them and they me. They loved the kids. Life was good. Space, however, was limited and Malc and I and the kids had to share one bedroom and keep praying for a council house of our own. (Such aspirations.) Long before the prayer was answered, Malc fell in love with a bus conductress and they set up home together, while the kids and I went back to live with my Pop. He had aged considerably over the last few months, and though he protested he was fit, healthy and perfectly capable of taking care of the kids while I got a job, I had my doubts.

I tried putting the boys in nursery school, but they screamed the place down. It broke my heart, I just couldn't leave them. The only alternative was a night job. I became a croupier – starting work at 11 p.m. and finishing at 5 a.m. After struggling through umpteen games of blackjack, I would taxi home and sleep till 8 a.m. when the boys awoke. A nap with them after lunch and bed with them at 7 p.m. till 10 made life all work and sleep, but the money was good.

As it turned out, I was a dreadful croupier and after a few weeks they put me on coats and hats. One evening, the usual sudden lull of conversation heralded the entrance of Johnny 'B' and his wife. Johnny 'B' was the local hood and hard man. Shef-field was his territory and he carried a 'piece' under his im-maculate Barney Goodman mohair. His 'Caesar' hair-cut was brilliantined into kiss-curls framing a face that had nasty carved all over it, and rumour had it that people who crossed him were never seen again.

His wife looked like a film star and sounded like a docker, and on their previous visits I'd managed to remain invisible while checking in her mink and his Crombie. Tonight was no ex-ception, as she gazed through me and he presented his broad, squat back and bald spot. They swaggered into the casino leaving me to settle down to my sewing – trousers for Lee – within the confines of my little kiosk. Suddenly a huge, hairy, knuckled hand bearing a diamond pinkie ring and a fiver appeared be-tween me and my sewing. It was Johnny 'B'.

'That's for your taxi fare tomorrow,' he said, dropping the money into my lap.

'That's O.K., the firm pays for my taxi,' I babbled, holding it out to him between trembling fingers as if it were a dead insect. He leaned over the counter and, resting on one elbow, slowly closed a huge hand over mine and the fiver, tightening his grip.

'I'm taking you out for lunch, darlin'. Meet me at 1 o'clock in Fitzalan Square. I'll drive us out to the Sun, we'll eat, then we'll fuck!'

'I think you might be a bit too subtle for me, Mr B,' I gasped, and at last he loosened his grip.

'Be there – or you'll really *get fucked*,' he hissed, jabbing a manicured index finger at my face and transfixing me with life-less black eyes. Then he turned and casually sauntered back to the gaming room. I was terrified. I grabbed the fiver and ran and never returned to the casino again. I lived in fear of him finding out where I lived. I was due in court in a few days to begin divorce proceedings and the threat of Johnny 'B' helped to dilute the worry. I hadn't seen Malc for some months.

7

Saturday 12 November

Today I met the faith healer Ronnie Hazlehurst recommended. I've always believed in God (**and Father Christmas**). Though raised Church of England, I rarely join the congregation since learning at the age of five that, according to the Church of England bible, God punished the naughty. With my track record, I thought it wise to keep out of His way.

I used to talk to Him on the wireless – still do sometimes. It works like this. You have to think of your problem for two days, then when the time feels right, switch on the radio and within five minutes if you listen intently the answer will pop out of the speakers.

I was fascinated by our shiny mahogany Sobell wireless set as a kid, and would wait hours for Dick Barton to emerge from the back. After a year or so of disappointment, my Dad gently explained about air waves, and I reasoned that if Dick Barton could send his voice through the air waves, God certainly could. He was a busy man, of course, and you couldn't waste his time with trivia; it had to be a major problem.

Old Mrs Gardner, who ran the post office and general store – the only shop in the small Scottish village – knew where most of Mom's widow's pension went and suggested I should persuade her to sign a consent form, allowing me to collect the pension. I could then buy food and give Mom the change, so ensuring we ate adequately. My problem for God was, how did I get her to sign the form? I thought about it for the prescribed two days, chanting, 'How do I get her to sign the form? – How do I get her to sign the form?', then switched on the wireless in the middle of a biblical play about Moses and God's voice boomed out of the speakers:

'TAKE THE TABLETS! TAKE THE TABLETS OF STONE DOWN THE MOUNTAIN AND GIVE THEM TO THE PEOPLE.'

I was awestruck. Of course! 'Take the tablets.' I hid her precious sleeping pills for two days till she signed the form, and we ate for a while.

It's worked on several occasions since, though never again in 'God's' voice. So you can see why I was open-minded about the faith healer. She's a friend of Bertice Reading, who is working at the Prince of Wales Theatre, so I arranged to meet her at the stage door at 2 o'clock. Her name is Dee.

Pam has come down for a day of shopping, bringing along our adopted younger sister Kath. Kath is a pretty dark-haired vivacious girl, whose flashing black eyes warn of the mass of complexities bubbling beneath the surface.

Shopping with them is expensive, exhausting and fun. I left them in the self-induced bedlam of a Harvey Nichols changing room, and promised to meet them later at the flat to examine our spoils, then went to meet Dee.

An attractive smartly dressed blonde in her forties stepped out of the doorway as my taxi drew to the kerb and she climbed in beside me. The taxi nosed its way back into the traffic as she introduced herself with a soft Cockney accent and a shy manner. She radiated warmth and we chatted easily on the ride back to the flat, then sat shoeless on the floor in front of the gas-fire, swapping husband humour and sipping coffee. When she felt the time was right, she took the cushions from the couch, arranged them on the floor and asked me to lie face down. I felt a bit stupid at first. She knelt beside me, saying nothing, and tapped three times on my back; I had to resist the urge to ask in a Boris Karloff voice: 'Is there anybody there?'

Dee's intense concentration soon settled me down. She placed featherlight hands on my back and shoulders. I began to relax. I didn't know what I expected (**chanting and rune casting, perhaps**), but I wasn't prepared for the tingling sensation affecting the areas of my body immediately underneath her small hands. Her touch became lighter until all I could feel was the heat radiating from her palms. Was it imagination? I was fully clothed, how come I could feel the warmth through my sweater? (**Don't question it, just accept.**) I decided to lie back and let it happen, and put it down to 'supernature'; I've witnessed it before.

The girls returned just as Dee was finishing. I'm glad Ronnie told me about her; I won't feel so stupid next time; the whole thing had a quiet dignity about it and I felt good.

After Dee left, we emptied the contents of our shiny carriers on to the floor and sat amid the jumble drinking coffee and trying on various 'finds' for each other's approval, between 'oohs' and 'aahs'.

While we waited for Pam to repack her carrier-bags (she always ends up with twice as many as anyone else) I tried unsuccessfully to force my size sevens into a pair of Kath's size fives. I love shoes and have boxes of worn-out pairs I can't bear to part with. (They say that's a sign of insecurity.) It's nice to have more than one pair.

Water oozed through the sodden cardboard inner soles, hastily fitted over the holes in my cheap plastic shoes as I stood in the rain outside the courtroom. This alone would have been sufficient grounds for divorce as far as my Pop was concerned.

As a kid my Pop had me measured and fitted into Kiltie or Start-Rite lace-ups, which despite my protests I wore until I was 16, feeling stupid at school hops and the youth club when all the other girls were in strappy sandles or black velvet 'boppers'. I was allowed to wear high heels for beauty contests, however, and when I started work, he always bought me expensive Italian leather.

Misreading the crumpled instructions I took the steps to the first floor, realised I should be on the fourth, so ran and eased myself through the closing lift doors, coming face to face with Malc.

We couldn't wait to get each other's clothes off.

We rode to the fourth floor, the doors slid open, we regarded each other in silence from our chosen corners, the doors slid to, and by the time we returned to the ground floor divorce was forgotten and the marriage reconsummated. (*Proving the old Yorkshire maxim: 'Keep her well shagged and poorly shod and she'll never leave you.'*)

By this time, Malc's Gran was living with his parents and the rift between him and Pop was too great to overcome, so we lived separately until we found an over-priced flat in a none too salubrious area of Sheffield. Less money, more women, more fights, another split. I piled the kids and what few possessions we had into the pram and, balancing the baby bath on the hood, walked the few miles back to my Pop's house. Sheffield, like Rome, is built on seven hills and I had to cross most of them, anger fuelling my journey as I thought of all the excuses I'd swallowed.

He was late because 'the police pulled me in to form part of an identity parade.' I believed him.

'That wasn't perfume on my jacket, Sheffield Transport has started using Estee Lauder's "Youth Dew" as air freshener.' I believed him.

'Yes, I know you're on the Pill; those condoms were planted on me, and God knows how they made their way under the linoleum in the upstairs closet.' Even that I believed, but the lipstick on his underpants 'administered by a gay dwarf in drag, brushing past me in the men's showers' was a bit much.

The postman handed me a letter as I eventually reached my Pop's house – it was an offer of a council house. Together again.

I often asked myself why I stayed around. I came up with these answers:

Firstly – he was an instinctive father, always concerned about his cubs, and as a seventeen-year-old handled his newborn son with the firm gentle confidence of an experienced midwife. Something permanent happened to my heart when I watched him, a tough street kid, cooing over his offspring. It was the beginning of a love far deeper than he ever realised. He always had time for them, always listened and was always reasonable with them. On the rare occasions serious chastisement was called for, he was the one who meted it out, never in anger, always in privacy after deep discussion with the culprit. With the boys he was reliable, dependable and consistent, a proper parent, and, while I refuse to whip myself any longer with the thought that I was a bad mother, I will admit to being unconventional. I'm aware of having made only two conscious sacrifices for the sake of my young, and neither of them has paid off. I made myself eat liver – they hate liver – and I gave up the odd episode of 'Coronation Street' to read them Rudyard Kipling – with actions and funny voices. Not only do they not remember the actions and funny voices, but, when asked if they even knew who Rudyard Kipling was, Max said: 'Of course we do, Mom – the Iranians are trying to assassinate him.'

Lee said, 'No. That's Willie Rushton.'

We share a good rapport. We could always make each other laugh. I kept them clean and well-dressed, made sure they ate the right things, had regular dental checks and all that, but some of my methods were unorthodox for the time. Our discussions were perhaps too frank and our jokes too smutty. I made them wash and iron and do certain cleaning jobs to earn their spending money. I taught them to cook, which my Mom-in-law thought demeaning for boys. Limited as my graces are, I was a stickler for manners and etiquette, which my Dad-in-law thought of as 'turnin' 'em into poofs'. I was quite tough with them and, though I've only ever smacked them once – with the stick end of a feather duster which, since reading Mommie Dearest, they've turned into a wire coat-hanger – I would often destroy them with tongue-lashings that still twist my conscience today.

If they were good they had a choice: share a banana split, or a trip to the pet shop to watch the gerbils screw. So you can see how much they needed Malc's stabilising influence.

The second reason I needed Malc was sex. We were so good at it. We practised endlessly, experimented, studied books, played games and climbed into each other's psyche with ease and without inhibition. We were familiar with each breath, each movement, each thought, and his extra-marital activities never diminished our mutual lust.

I never for a moment blamed Malc entirely. I was bolshie, bossy, impatient, ambitious and extremely strong-minded. My ego was massaged constantly by applause. To compete, I suppose, Malc had his ego (and other parts) massaged between the sheets and in my heart of hearts I knew his affairs were superficial – of the genitals rather than the heart – and during one of our deep analytical discussions on the subject, he admitted that he couldn't wait to leave his lover's bed and get home once the act was over.

I tried every trick in the book to reform him. Eventually it dawned on me that he wasn't going to change and I had the choice of either leaving or learning to live with it. I learned to live with it.

We decided the deception was the worst part of it and agreed to give honesty a try. His lying was pointless anyway, I knew him too well. He always went for a type – dark-haired, dark-eyed endomorphs – and when chatting up his quarry, his voice would change from baritone to bass baritone without realising.

The honesty policy worked wonderfully. It took a lot of the fuel from his flames (the fruit no longer forbidden is no *longer desired). A great camaraderie and friendship evolved and miracle of miracles, he settled down for some years before a dark-haired, dark-eyed endomorph stole his heart for good.*

Pam and Kath followed me back to the cottage, where we sat in front of a **smoking** log fire and gossiped and giggled till bed-time.

It's the charity fashion show tomorrow: The London Hilton, 7 o'clock. I've decided to add my own gown to the auction as it's for a good cause, Guy's Hospital cancer unit. I suppose I benefit indirectly. It's a bit like being a road-builder with a brother on the council. With that in mind, I selected my favourite gown – a black silk 'Spanish' job with roses under the flared cap-sleeves. **(Nina once said you looked as though you were renting your armpits out as allotments.)** I filled the bath with hot water and hung the frock above the steam to let the creases drop out overnight.

8

It's the final of 'New Faces '88' and the theatre is crack-ling with excitement. Sound engineers, lighting techni-cians, set designers, carpenters and electricians have been working night and day, high on the adrenalin that 90 minutes of live T.V. induces. There's a stretch-steel tension in the normally soothing make-up room, where nine intently concentrating make-up girls are tending the terrified contestants – and this is only a dress-run. Admittedly there's an audience. We have to try out the master scoreboard, a slick computerised monster and a change from the usual 'Spaghetti Junction', so need the audience to check the theatre's voting system.

The contestants are always attended to first. I slip into make-up whenever and wherever there's a spare chair, and today Lynette Braid, head of the department, is the miracle worker who paints out the dots and dashes and lines and circles.

'What's this, Mart?'

She's found a lump on my neck – a small one about the size of a marble – that wasn't there last time she powdered that bit. Since I stopped taking the chlorambucil, the lumps are beginning to return, which is just as well. We've been in touch with Stanford who will accept me if my lymphoma is of the right type. To determine this they want to do their own biopsy, and will require a sizeable lymph node to go at.

Hairdressers and make-up artists know who's had what done and where, who's had whom, when and how, and with what, where and how many times, and in the thirteen years I've known Lynette, I have never known her betray a confidence, so I tell her what the lump is.

She barely has time to recover before Nina Myskow breezes in with a smile that makes her look like a 10-year-old (**a ten-year-old Stilton, that is**), hurls her customary, 'Hello, you old bag,' and her reflection kisses the air beside my cheek. She's looking good in a loose black silk jacket with a huge jewelled Butler and Wilson spider climbing the lapel.

'What's that horrendous creature you have about your person?' I ask.

'It's a spider.'

'I was *talking* to the spider!' We decide to try that one out on the audience. The badinage between Nina and myself is never rehearsed, but this is live T.V. and we need all the help we can get.

Taxi-drivers, autograph hunters, friends and family alike are curious about our offstage relationship, and wonder whether our heated exchanges are continued after the show. No, I rarely see her after the show. Not being a drinker, I do an obligatory flip round the post-show party, consoling or congratulating and giving what little advice I can to grieving or glowing parents. Then I return to my suite at the Albany Hotel to sit out the adrenalin hangover. Nina, on the other hand, parties all night, often until it is time to catch the 9 a.m. train to London.

I become totally involved with the contestants on 'New Faces'. A strong maternal instinct takes over. For the two days of the show I cluck round them – soothing, calming, encouraging and reassuring. I guard them like a mother tiger, and when Nina starts to tear into them I could cheerfully strangle her, and it shows. She's fast, caustic and intelligent, but she also has a vulnerability, easy to spot, even under the 'Wicked Witch of Wapping' image, and off-stage it is her my instinct tells me to protect and defend.

Nina tends to voice what many people are thinking. If the performer can't stand the heat at this stage of their career, we're doing no favours pushing them into the kitchen. As for the survivors, they leave with thickened skin and renewed determination.

Nina knows about the lymphoma; I had to cancel a prearranged lunch at Langans with her as it coincided with my short stay in hospital, and rather than make up an excuse I thought it an opportune time to tell her. She was too upset to continue the call and I regretted my decision.

My bone marrow was harvested a couple of weeks ago and the whole thing was a piece of cake. I awoke in the soundproofed luxury of the Princess Grace Hospital, none the worse for the two-hour operation. A couple of gauze dressings covered the small twin holes either side of my spine, and all that remains today are two little scabs and a few bruises. I felt a little stiff, but perfectly well. I was surprised how weak and light-headed I felt on nipping out of my hospital bed to recover a dropped book. I figured my body was telling me to rest, so I've flopped around for the last two weeks eating steaks and drinking beef tea, and getting stronger every day. I kept my schedule light: one cheque presentation, one dental appointment, one fitting for the Red Queen crown, and a last visit to Dr McKenzie before the panto rehearsals start on Monday. He said the scars from the bone-marrow harvest were healing nicely. The lumps, he noted, were returning with a slow vengeance and he confirmed that nonetheless I should be able to fulfil the requirements of a demanding panto season with no trouble.

I had an unsettling experience on Thursday. I drove to the Birmingham Hippodrome in time for the 11 o'clock production meeting with the contestants. The atmosphere became charged within minutes of their arrival and the day was spent in frantic dashes, nerve-shattering band calls, fraught costume fittings and in-furiating sound checks, so by the time I booked into my Albany Hotel suite at 6 o'clock I felt exhausted. I had arranged to meet Howard Imber, the writer, for a script conference over dinner at 8, and fell on to the bed in-tending to rest for ten minutes before reading through the thick camera script.

It was 7.45 when I opened my eyes and I couldn't move. My head, arms and legs felt buried under tons of sand and my torso felt strapped to the mattress. I was soaked in perspiration and the muscles running the length of my spine were in spasm.

I was scared. (**Calm down.**) This was no ordinary

tiredness, this was more like paralysis. Was it a symptom? Was this how it would be? **(Remember what Joe said about imagination!)** I had to cancel the script conference. I tried to reach for the phone to ring Howard, but my arm refused to move. **(You'll feel better when you've eaten.)** I lay on the bed for what seemed like hours, sweating and totally helpless, trying to will myself to move. **(Get off your arse and into that shower, you sap!)** With monumental effort I crawled into the shower and soon began to feel better. I arrived ten minutes later for dinner with Howard and was completely recovered by the end of the meal. I'm still wondering whether the experience was physiological or psychological.

Sunday 4 December – 5 A.M.

I'm watching a silent T.V. The flickering light from the screen changes the mood of the dark room every few seconds, but I'm impervious to mood. I can't see, or hear, or laugh, or cry. I am numb, suffering from an adrenalin hangover. They seem to get worse as I get older. I feel like a Polo Mint, a thick, brittle wall surrounding a void that used to be me. Kenneth is sleeping soundly in the bedroom half of the suite, but it's pointless joining him, my eyes won't close. It's always like this after a show, an anticlimactic darkness, and I wish I was a typist. **(No, you don't.)**

The movie on T.V. is reaching its climax and even without sound, it's clear the hero is innocent. The heroine has escaped and alerted the police, who at the last minute burst in and save our hero from a fate worse than death. The villain makes a run for it, knocking over

an oil-lamp and setting fire to his evil lair, and the titles
drift past a close-up of his silent scream and melting face.
I think how unlike the real thing it is.

The routine of life as a young mother was interrupted occasion-
ally by visits from the police informing me that my Mother had
taken an overdose and was in hospital being 'pumped-out'. I'd
fetch her home, clean her up, straighten her out and take care of
her for as long as she'd let me, but the call of the wild was strong
and after a few days of sleeping on the couch, she'd vanish again.

It was no great shock, therefore, when around the time of
my nineteenth birthday, the police informed me she was in hospi-
tal again. Dropping the kids off at my mother-in-law's, I trudged
the few miles to the hospital taking the short cut through the
grounds to the usual ward. She wasn't there. I was informed she
was in the burns unit.

The sister in charge of the unit was expecting me, and when
I arrived, led me into her office. After confirming that I wasn't
taking any medication, she gave me two small white pills with a
glass of water and sat me down, explaining that my Mother had
been seriously burned and the pills were to help me with the
shock when I saw her.

I waited in the office for an hour before she led me into a
darkened side ward.

A saline drip stood like the Angel of Death beside the bed, a
pipe leading to one of her arms which lay by her side atop neatly
folded sheets. A white cloth had been placed over her unpillowed
head hiding her injuries, but the room was filled with an over-
powering stench like smouldering wool.

'Is that you, flower?' she asked in a muffled, but normal
voice.

Surprised, I said: 'Yes. What happened?'

She waited until she heard the sister leave before telling me.

She had taken a handful of downers with her whisky around 10 a.m. and had woken up in hospital. Whoever she was living with, roused by the smell of burning, had come downstairs to discover her slumped across the hearth with her head pressed up against a glowing electric fire.

Oddly enough, she wasn't in pain when she came round, and she said she didn't know what they'd shot into her, but she felt great and wished she could score some. They'd put her into a side ward and removed the mirrors and she asked me to peek under the cloth and tell her what she looked like.

Her head was three times its normal size, one huge, crusty, black blister, her eyes like two slit tennis balls, and the lower half of her face seemed to have no features at all except enormous fat black lips that covered her nostrils and chin. I replaced the cover gently.

'Well?'

'Not as bad as I thought it would be,' I lied.

I saw the doctor on the way out. He told me she'd lost an ear, carbonized the top of her skull and badly damaged the right side of her face. Burns, he said, were rarely the cause of death, though the resulting shock-induced pneumonia was. As she was drugged up to the eyeballs on arrival, she hadn't yet gone into shock but they were expecting it and, if she survived, then miracles could be performed.

She did survive. They grew a new 'ear' on her stomach with grafts taken from her thighs; the scab on the superficially burnt left side of her face lifted off almost in one piece, leaving behind the flawless pink skin of a teenager; but even after a year in hospital and scores of painful grafts, the right side of her face was hideously scarred, her hair and eyebrows never grew again and a plastic plate fitted over her carbonized skull prevented her from wearing a wig.

She walked with a stagger, due to damage to the middle

ear, her head swathed in a bandage and saliva dripping from the disfigured side of her mouth. She became an object of ridicule. No amount of persuasion would induce her to stay with us for more than a few days before she'd vanish again to pursue her old habits, and on New Year's Day 1967, the police called for the last time.

The show went smoothly. Everything and everybody worked well and on cue. By now, winners or losers, the contestants will be sleeping or coping with their own adrenalin hangover in their own way, and it feels like my chicks have left the nest. The extraordinary circumstances of the last three days have bound us together for a minimum of eighteen hours a day, breakfast, lunch and dinner, and we've got to know each other well.

The tension and excitement built gradually all day and the dress-run audience caught the vibes and responded, making every artist want to give more. The secret is holding it in check, rationing it, saving the best of yourself for the night, and as I scanned the running order in the lull before the storm, I still couldn't decide on a personal favourite.

Dennie Hodge, the best warm-up man in the business, was front of tabs having an easy time with an exuberant audience, and Harry Rabinowitz was studying the gentlemen of his orchestra as they settled themselves, checking notes, swapping jokes and generally tuning in to the excitement.

Keith Lascelles, friend and floor manager, turned from his prompt side console and, raising one enquiring eyebrow, asked: 'Miss Caine?' – not needing to add, 'Shall I tell Dennie you're ready to meet your public and to take over the warm-up for ten minutes?'

I nodded and he turned back to mutter something into his talkback before handing me the mike, taking my hand and leading me to the stage. The audience were a comic's dream and when Dennie came back on stage and whispered 'two minutes to count-down' I ran off to applause that made me feel like Mike Tyson.

My heart was beating in my throat making it hard to swallow, my nose was running, my hands were cold and I couldn't get enough oxygen, which made me yawn every few seconds.

'ONE MINUTE AND COUNTING' breathed a reasonable tannoy.

I was standing in the wings on prompt side amid the varicosed tangle of cables webbing the black stage. I checked my reflection once more in the dimly lit mirror and a sea of faces misted out behind me.

'THIRTY SECONDS – STAND BY'

Keith Lascelles took my hand, squeezing it reassuringly as he led me across the stage, up the wide stairway dividing the orchestra, and left me to arrange myself on the rostrum. The gentlemen of the orchestra chorused their usual soft whistles of approval and I did my usual twirl, deep curtsey and, 'Good evening, gentlemen.'

'Good evening, Miss Caine.'

''Ere, Mart ...' second trumpet, ' ... would you object to waking up with green elbows and knees?'

'No,' I oblige.

'Do you wanna come campin'?' We all laugh.

''Ere, Mart ...' second trumpet again.

'Yes?'

'Somebody bought Stevie Wonder a cheese grater for Christmas and he said it was the most violent novel he'd ever read!' We all laugh again.

''Ere, Mart . . .' 'TEN-NINE-EIGHT–' Stomach in, shoulders back. Relax. Relax. 'FIVE-FOUR' Oh, my God! Who's on first? Drum roll . . .'

'. . . welcome the host of the show – MISS MARTI CAINE!' I spun into the spotlight with arms raised, smile flashing, galloped down the stairs, trying not to look down, across the stage, bowing like a courting duck to the boxed panel en route, along the promontory jutting out into the midst of the wildly cheering audience and, as the extravagant applause began at last to subside, heard myself say:

'Good evening and welcome to the Grand Final of "New Faces '87".'

It's been '88 for almost a year. (**Things can only get better.**)

Blessed with a good audience there's always a danger of the comics running overtime, and it's up to me to stretch or speed up the show should the need arise. We've stressed the importance of 'inner-clock discipline' and all the contestants stick within their time boundaries. With the help of Keith Lascelles and Howard Imber, I closed the first hour of the show within thirty seconds of the allocated time. (**At least you've done something right.**)

The winner in the theatre was Stephen Lee Garden, a clean-cut handsome young singer with a beautiful voice and an earnest, open face. The camera loved him. There's only half an hour intermission while the news is on and the votes are collated, and the contestants' fear ferments into an almost hysterical euphoria.

I slid the last of the three jackets over the plain black sheath, re-glossed my lips, re-spiked my hair and '. . . THREE-TWO-ONE-ROLLING–' we're back on air.

For the next half-hour I rattled the results as they came in from local stations all over the country. The expensive, state-of-the-art scoreboard ablur with speeding rows of changing numbers and names confirmed my announcements at the speed of light, and the almost unanimous winner was Stephen Lee Garden.

There was a riotous party afterwards. Mixed with surplus adrenalin, even coffee can be inebriating so the revellers became merry, very quickly. Somebody's Mom wanted her programme signed, somebody's Gran wanted a photograph and somebody's Aunty Val wanted to strangle Nina Myskow.

That was the last show of the series and I feel sad it's over.

No time to brood, rehearsals for the panto begin tomorrow.

9

Tuesday 6 December
Cambidge

It's the opening night of 'Snow White' at the Cambridge Arts Theatre and backstage excitement is mounting. The 20-ft-square Green Room is walled with dressing rooms full of Snow White, Prince Charming, the Narrator, the Gipsy Queen, Catsmeat – the Red Queen's familiar – and eight of the Seven Dwarfs. (Class production – some shows have three dwarfs and four cardboard cut-outs.) I declined the isolated 'star' dressing room on the floor above, preferring to be with my fellows. My door, like everyone else's, remains open.

Impervious to the babble of conversation and the pop music blaring from the dancers' dressing room, I stick the exaggerated lashes in place, put on my spectacular Medusa-like crown and walk through the Green Room to the coffee-making area. Wardrobe are seated round a huge dish of communal sweets on the Green

Room table, sewing Freddie Fox's tail in place, while Bertie Badger, the children's favourite, complains: 'I can't see a fucking thing in this head-dress!'

Six pom-poms glide past the end of the table and we realise that one of the dwarves has lost his hat.

Two of the musicians, carrying the usual cans of Gold Label, pop their heads in and shout: 'Break a leg, gang.'

'Merde,' we chorus back, feeling terribly 'thespian'.

It's hot, it's happy and it's home for the next six weeks, along with the University Arms Hotel a few minutes' walk away. Kenneth drove me here last Sunday after helping me to load the car with clothes, shoes, video recorder, sound equipment, books, photos, kettle, mug, hot-water-bottle (**never go anywhere without it**) and all the required paraphernalia of a season away from home.

The hotel staff were wonderful, coping with the unusual load with quiet, efficient speed and within half an hour I was installed, my possessions absorbed into cupboards and a free-standing rail supplied to accommodate my surplus clothes.

After lunch we explored Cambridge, mindless of the cold drizzle, appreciating the contrast of mellow stone pitched against a pencilled sky. Thrusting spires, softened by time; vaulted cloisters floored with cobbles trod thin by genius. Jewel-bright windows, veiled in lead, gaze on slender arched bridges across the Cam.

Narrow alleys streak out from a market square, gay with canopy stripes, bookshops, boutiques, steamy little tea-shops, hat-shops, shoe-shops, curio- and card-shops, all pressed together, closing ranks to thousands of cyclists. Cambridge is a beautiful city.

The rehearsals went well from square one, and we become a family at once; the dwarves, initially shy and insular, quickly joined us. I've worked hard on the 'proper English' accent and with Kenneth's help, got rid of the Yorkshire 'u' sound – as in bus – but had a little trouble with the 'ay' sound – as in fade. Finally he drummed it out of me and, satisfied at last, congratulated me on my efforts. I'm glad he wasn't at the dress-run last night when, in my most imperious Dame Edith voice, I commanded, 'Send for Hedward the Hugly!' and Edward the Ugly fell off the stage laughing.

I haven't told the management about the lymphoma, and haven't had a repeat of the weakness I experienced in Birmingham, so have put it down to adrenalin overdose and imagination. The lumps are slowly getting bigger and I have a new one at the top of my leg, the size of a pullet's egg. It would have shown through the 'New Faces' sheath dress.

The weather was fine this morning and after a full English breakfast, Kenneth accompanied me on the leisurely stroll to the theatre. A woman of about 30 lurched out of the Post Office in front of us and staggered down the road a few steps before falling – her exposed thighs and palms making a sickening 'slap-smack' sound on the pavement. She was obviously under the influence of drugs, booze or both and as we approached, typically averting our eyes from the embarrassing spectacle, a girl of about 11 wiped a candle of yellow mucus from the woman's nose and resignedly helped her to her feet, staring at us with old, resentful eyes as we passed, reminding me of myself and the Saturday afternoon rescue missions. I wondered what would become of them both.

It was Dad (as I now knew Malc's father) who opened the door at 6.45 p.m. on the first day of 1967. We were staying with my in-laws and were all invited to a New Year party by the Wragg family next door but one.

I looked down at my sweet-smelling rosy babies, newly bathed and attired for the night in matching Christmas pyjamas and fluffy slippers. They were fascinated by the entrails of the 'Chuffa-chuffa-clang-clang' train strewn over the hearthrug as Malc and a screwdriver attempted to revive this sole survivor of Christmas.

Malc was taking first watch with the kids and was in no hurry to leave the cosy guarded fireside for the icy wastes of the bathroom. His cross-legged knees were toasting nicely, poking from beneath the towelling robe as he bent, absorbed, over his task.

A gruff baritone 'Malcolm!' broke the spell as Dad's head appeared round the door and jerked a 'Come here' in Malc's direction.

My stomach gave an involuntary lurch. A prickling sensation between my eyes made my nose run and white-hot adrenalin scalded the subcutaneous layer beneath my skin. Something was terribly wrong. Lee picked up the vibes and looked with wide-eyed apprehension as I held my breath and waited.

Malc reappeared round the door, looked at me over the top of his specs and reached out and I walked towards his out-stretched arms on liquid legs. He folded me into his body and putting his lips against my hair, whispered, 'Your Mom died, Lynne.'

I felt nothing. I watched the events unfold like a screen play, staring dry-eyed at the projected image of two policemen, stiff with duty, beyond the open door and Dad sitting, head in hands, on the stairs. A bloodsoaked snatch of toilet tissue drifted in slow motion from the shaving nick on his jaw and touched down, a wounded flake, on the door-mat. A January wind forced an entry through the legs of the law – eagerly sniffed the corners of the hall, wafted aside Malc's dressing gown and pressed itself through my home-made dress to conduct an icy-handed body search.

A distant voice chiselled its way into my consciousness and fell in fragments:

' . . . was found in the early hours of this morning . . . suspect an overdose . . . post mortem . . . need you to identify the body . . . 10 o'clock tomorrow . . .' The younger policeman shuffled in embarrassment under my glassy gaze as the elder one continued to recite the report from a notebook in his mind.

Dad rose, and closed the door on their retreat and the unthinking 'Happy New Year!' from the younger officer. Dad was a gruff bear of a Yorkshire man, warm but not tactile, his rare hugs self-conscious, one-armed and brief, but the compassion in his eyes was overwhelming as he placed his large hands on my shoulders and murmured: 'Ah, lass, lass.'

The feeling of numb unreality persisted and anaesthetised me through the arduous business of identifying the body and making the necessary arrangements. I didn't begin to feel again until anger kissed me back to life at the inquest.

Dr Pilling, the Coroner, recorded an open verdict. Though my Mother had enough barbiturates in her system to kill ten people, her addiction had built up sufficient tolerance to suggest the possibility of an accidental overdose. He noted that she'd had numerous stomach pumps as a result of such accidents in the past, and someone should have cared.

I despised his fat-cat complacency. His podgy, clean-nailed fingers locked together and formed a vaulted shrine over the few pages of notes that contained my Mother's life. He'd become acquainted with her only hours before the hearing and would forget her minutes afterwards. His life was a million miles away from ours, his past revered, his future assured, the son of a doctor and the father of one, and when it came to 'caring' he'd only touched the surface.

It was only to Pam that I admitted to feeling guilty and ashamed of the wave of relief I felt at her funeral, as though a weight had been lifted from my shoulders. Yet I loved her so much and not a day goes past without a thought of her.

My Mother wasn't insured and the funeral director's bill of £150 was a shock (he might as well have asked for the moon). I had to find the money somewhere. The bill had arrived just before our fifth wedding anniversary, celebrated with a rare night out at the Working Men's Club with my in-laws and Pam and her first husband, Gordon. The debt played on my mind as I half listened to a soprano trying to sing Lulu's 'Shout'. (Maria Callas sings Little Richard.) Having finished her spot, the soprano left the stage and rejoined her husband and the Concert Secretary who were sitting at the next table. I watched in disbelief as the Con-Sec paid her, counting out the notes and thumbing them from a pile on to the table in front of her so that all could witness his honesty.

Seven pounds, he paid her – SEVEN POUNDS! That was more than half of Malc's entire weekly wage and the answer to our problems. I bought myself three copies of music and Malc and I trotted off to Chapeltown Working Men's Club where a local agent, Ernest 'Honest' Johns, held weekly auditions.

As I handed my music to the organist, I shook so badly he bought me a brandy and made me drink it. Every mouthful made me heave, but I forced it down and chased it with a second one bought by Malc. I began to feel better and weaved my way on to the stage after the third intro of 'Puppet on a String'. My knees were knocking and my lips quivering, making it difficult to get round the words. My voice was trembling so much, I sounded like Edith Piaf with Parkinson's disease. The organist and I finished more or less together and I turned to him for reassurance as I announced my next song: 'And now, "Summer Time".'

As the organist began the introduction, the lights dimmed to add 'mood', allowing me my first sight of the sparse audience. My throat closed, I felt sick, I couldn't breathe and when my voice finally squawked out, I realised the song was far too high for me. I changed down an octave on ' . . . time, and the living is eas . . .' and up again on '. . . sy."

It was terrible. I stopped until an urgent, 'Go on, lass, go on, you're doin' fine,' from the organist prompted the next line. I could now see Malc on the front row quite clearly. His face was stricken and he was mouthing the lyrics and making Shirley Bassey gestures in an effort to will me into continuing. I finished the song and only as I left the stage did I realise I had wet myself with fear. Ernest 'Honest' Johns approached us as we slunk out of the club.

'You'll do. Get yourself twelve songs – and have them transposed into the right key, for God's sake. Your first gig is on Sunday – a noon and night at Aldwarke Road Working Men's Club, Rawmarsh. Seven quid – I want 10%, O.K.? Ring me and let me know how you do.'

Our fear was forgotten. Seven quid! We'd found a gold mine. I borrowed forty pounds from Malc's Mum and bought myself a long black frock with diamanté trim and began to learn my trade. The fear got worse and when it reached the stage where five brandies were required to get me on stage, I had to stop and take stock of myself. I had no desire to inflict an alcoholic parent on MY children. The next night I went on without Dutch courage and flattened a drunken heckler with a couple of speedy put-downs that came from nowhere ('twas I, your valiant defence mechanism again) and a new career was born.

I wasn't Marti Caine at that stage, I was Zoe Bond, but only after being Sunny Smith for three weeks. I didn't want to be a

'Julie Rose' or a 'Cindy Summers', I wanted a name like Kiki Dee or Dusty Springfield and didn't feel 'Zoe Bond' was quite 'it'. We took a book from a shelf, which happened to be a gardening book.

'O.K. – page seventy-six.' Malc turned to the required page.

'Fourth line down, second word along'

'Greenfly.'

'O.K. Page thirty four ...' and so on until, bored with the game, Malc came across. 'Tomato cane – that'll do, you're built like one. Call yourself Marta Cane.'

I rang the club I was appearing at and informed the Con-Sec that Marta Cane would be appearing in place of Zoe Bond who was ill. When I arrived at the club, I found I was billed (in coloured chalk) as Marti Caine. I liked it.

Within six months, I'd repaid the forty-pound loan from my mom-in-law. I incurred a second funeral director's bill the same week as I paid off the first. My Pop had died, peacefully, after a heart attack.

He'd seen me working only once. He was quite impressed, but said I should be a comic. Shortly after his death, I was working a 'noon and night' at a local Working Men's Club when the top of the bill – a Welsh comic called Dave Swan – was unable to do the evening performance, as he'd been taken ill.

I had almost total recall when it came to gags, and innocently told the Con-Sec that as it was too late to engage a replacement comic, I'd gladly do Dave Swan's act for him, and went on to storm the audience.

Mass adoration is a highly addictive drug. I was hooked, I knew my singing wasn't good enough to evoke that kind of reaction from an audience. The only way to do it was as a comic. But as the Con-Sec pointed out, while paying me an extra two quid for stepping into the breach, I couldn't pinch Dave Swan's act. I had to have one of my own.

I set about building up an act with the aid of Rag maga-zines, joke-books, a gag nicked from here, a gag nicked from there and at my next engagement, four days later, I was billed as a comic and my fee went up a few quid.

I gained confidence, improved my delivery, added to my re-pertoire and became quite cocky until I suffered my first 'death'. Then I realised why comics earn more money than singers.

It was another Sunday noon show – in Leeds, Rainworth Social Club. The hangar-sized concert room was packed with a well-behaved male dominated audience. A family of brothers, fathers and uncles on the front table took an instant dislike to me and, slamming their pints on the table, sat back with arms crossed and regarded me in stony-faced silence. The mood spread backward, rolling down the room like a tidal wave of hostility, the sound of slamming beer mugs following in its wake. In the silence that followed I could hear the beer pumps hissing behind the bar at the back of the room.

'That's enough, lass,' said the chairman from his micro-phoned pulpit beside the stage and drew the curtains on me. I stepped through them, anger replacing fear and humiliation. I continued for fifty minutes, alienating the audience more with every gag, until I walked off to the sound of my own footsteps.

I was slow-hand-clapped out of the club and never re-booked. It took me quite a while to rebuild my confidence. None of my many subsequent 'deaths' were ever as bad as that first one. There's always the chance, though, that the next time I step on stage, it will be.

The lights dim and hushed expectancy shudders through the packed house. The band strikes up the overture and Clare, the assistant stage manager, sits in the cramped prompt corner, whispering urgent instructions to sound, lights and flymen.

First lighting condition is total black-out, geared to show off the lightning flashes of the opening act 'storm'. As the overture reaches 'Hi-Ho', I grope my way across the pitch-black stage until my outstretched hands make contact with a rostrum set centre-stage. Gathering my skirt and veils around me, I feel my way up five steps and stand ready, back to the audience, on the 2ft-square platform. The overture finishes to applause, the curtains open, thunder rumbles and lightning flashes to reveal me, arms raised skyward and apparently floating in mid-air, as a huge mirror silently descends and I speak the first lines:

> Mirror, Mirror, on the wall,
> Who is the fairest of them all?

The mirror tells me it's Snow White. I spin to face the audience, hands clawed, face contorted with fury, and in a voice stolen from *The Exorcist* reply:

> Snow White? Lies, lies, lies.

10

Saturday 17 December

At 10 o'clock this morning Clifford Elson, my press
agent, rang.

'Marti, the news is out. So far it's only in the *Daily
Mirror* and *Today*.'

Common sense told me the news would break
sooner or later, even if it wasn't until my funeral, so on
first being diagnosed, I had rung Clifford, with a statement to give to the press, should it become necessary, to
the effect that my job was to make people forget their
problems and not to talk about mine.

'Oh well, I suppose it was inevitable. I'm relieved in
a way. It's been hanging over my head like the sword of
Damocles. I'm glad it's over and done with.'

'It's not "over and done with" Marti. The whole of
Fleet Street are on their way up. Prepare yourself.'

The phone rang again as I replaced it. It was John
Sowden, the company manager, calling from the theatre.

'Mart? Listen, there are about forty journalists; as many photographers; Central T.V., Anglia T.V., Radio, the works, all waiting outside the stage door. What do you want to do?' (**A six-month tour of Australia, starting now.**)

'Avoid them.'

'Right. Come to the flower shop next to the front doors of the theatre. We'll be waiting.' I replaced the phone and it rang again immediately. Reception this time; would I care to leave through the underground garage rather than the front doors and so escape the army of press who were filling the lobby?

I thanked her for her consideration and said I would. Within seconds one of the porters was knocking at the door to escort us down in case of trouble. We sped from the car park undetected and screeched to a halt outside the flower shop, as instructed. A cordon of stagehands appeared from nowhere and surrounded me as I stepped out of the car. My feet barely touching the floor, they rushed me through a gate, up a small passage and into the theatre, avoiding an alerted, stampeding press by a split second.

The cast and crew gathered in the Green Room were dumb-struck. They had had no idea that anything was amiss. An awkward, almost embarrassed atmosphere hung over the normally happy room.

'I'm O.K., compared to the guy next door. He was given only three days to live. When he told his wife she said, "Right love, you can have anything you want for your tea – anything, you've only three days to live, what do you fancy?"

'"A nice bit of steak," he said and she rushed out and bought him a steak. Next night he fancied a bit of fresh salmon and as he only had two days to live, she rushed out and bought him some salmon. On his last day, feeling a little guilty about sending his wife out shopping, he said, "There's no need to go shopping today, love, I notice you have a nice bit of boiled ham in the fridge, I'll have that with a few tomatoes."

She said, "You can sod off! That's for the funeral tea tomorrow."'

Thus began a 30 minute gag-telling session, doctor gags, hospital gags and funeral gags, until we'd laughed away the atmosphere. We went on to do a good matinée performance and came off to thunderous applause and whistles of appreciation. (Or was it sympathy?) Performers are so insecure.

Returning to my dressing room, I removed my headdress and reached for a towel to dry my sweat-soaked hair – fighting with seven dwarfs under banks of spotlights is hot work. I'd allowed the door to swing to behind me and just as it clicked shut, someone knocked. Thinking it was my dresser I opened the door to find a *News of the World* journalist standing there. He'd ducked under the curtains and made his way to the dressing rooms via the stage.

I had to admire his nerve, but declined to answer any of his rushed questions, saying, 'Sorry – no comment,' and closed the door. I heard a scuffle outside and presumed he'd been escorted from the building, but before leaving he pushed a *News of the World* Christmas card under the door offering me £40,000 for an interview.

I always had a good relationship with the press. I was honest. I wouldn't insult their intelligence by lying and we had a healthy respect for each other. I needed them as much as they needed me and I happily took the rough with the smooth.

But over the past few years a new breed of journalist has evolved – hungry, competitive and aggressive. Unlike the 'old school', the new breed go for the jugular. Once, a joky quote would be reported in the manner in which it was delivered. Now it is fallen upon and twisted and embellished out of all recognition. Words are put into the mouths of the unwary, and thirty pieces of silver are offered to 'toy-boy' lovers, 'plaything' bimbos and ex-Royal servants. They have whetted a lust for sensationalism that has turned us into a nation of accident watchers.

Dodging the press wasn't going to be easy and Kenneth and I didn't leave the theatre until 1.30 a.m. when the all-clear was given by the wonderfully protective theatre staff.

Sunday 18 December

I was woken this morning by Kenneth throwing a pile of Sunday newspapers on to my eiderdowned feet. I opened my eyes and glowered at him. (**Vocal communication is out of the question till after the third cup of coffee.**)

'Have you seen the headlines?'

Grunt?

I struggled to a sitting position and he handed me the tabloids which had slipped from the end of the bed. I was horrified. I couldn't believe what I was reading:

Sunday Mirror – **'I'LL FIGHT FOR MY LIFE' SAYS MARTI**

I've never said anything of the sort to anyone – far less a

journalist.

Sunday People – **BRAVERY OF A REAL TROUPER**

Brave? I'm not brave, I'm scared stupid. I feel such a sham – coward is nearer the truth. I was sick of reading magazine and newspaper articles about 'brave fights' by various well-known personalities and didn't intend to become one of them. I'm no braver than Mrs Smith or Mr Jones, or 2-year-old Tommy, or *any* of the many people who have cancer.

News of the World – **'TRAGIC MARTI COLLAPSES ON STAGE'**

When? Where? I feel terrific. I've never collapsed – on stage or anywhere else.

Sitting up in bed, I scanned the article, which the *News of the World* claimed was an exclusive interview. Apparently not only had I collapsed on stage last night, but I was having intravenous chemotherapy between shows, sobbing and grimacing in agony in my dressing room.

It was a nightmare, anyone reading the papers would think I was on my last legs. I'll never work again. Where did they get their information? I haven't even told the majority of my friends yet. They'll be worried sick. I sat by the phone and rang as many of them as I could, reassuring the ones who were home.

Friday 23 December

It's been a very trying few days. Press and photographers continue to pursue us and we're virtually prisoners. The reaction has been overwhelming. I had absolutely no idea it would be this big. Moreover, I can't understand why some press still remain, because I steadfastly refuse to comment.

Kenneth finally lost his cool with a photographer this morning, and threatened to hit him. I was mortified. That's all we need – Kenneth arrested.

On the positive side, I feel fine physically and my spirits are being lifted immeasurably by the mail that's beginning to pour in. One letter was from an old customer of a café Malc and I once had. I was painfully thin at the time and he commented, 'We could almost touch your shoulder-blades as you dashed past with plates of chips.'

My career was flourishing. I had reached the dizzy heights of compère at the Fiesta, one of the North's most prestigious night clubs, where I did an hour spot and introduced acts like Ella Fitzgerald and Nancy Wilson, as well as all the top British acts. It gave me an opportunity to study the great comics like Tommy Cooper and Dave Allen, and to hone my skills as a singer with the band. Compèring is a specialised craft. You have to project sufficient ego to fill the room and control the crowd without intimidating the support acts, who are often less talented.

You have to be spontaneous. Many's the time I've been about to introduce the top of the bill, when from behind the curtain the urgent whisper, 'He's pissed – fill in while we sober him up,' has stopped me in my tracks and left me out there telling gags for an hour or more while the star is force-fed black coffee.

The Fiesta was as plush back-stage as it was out front. The 2000-strong audience wore full evening dress. It was how I'd always imagined showbiz would be – far removed from the stark reality of Working Men's Clubs.

The Working Men's Clubs had made me. They gave me the vitally important gift of being able to 'feel' an audience, a precious sixth sense that cannot be taught. The audiences often give honest, if unsolicited, criticism and advice (You're rubbish. Ger'off!) and the thought of returning to them once my Fiesta contract finished filled me with dread. I would lose my glass slipper. My beautiful evening gowns would turn into home-made minis. My chauffeur-driven car would turn into a Ford Escort with clutch trouble, and my flower-decked en-suite dressing room would turn into a nail in the wall. I couldn't bear being a pumpkin again. I decided we couldn't continue to rely on showbiz. I had to get out of the business.

To this end, Malc and I rented a shop in a local precinct and turned it into a café. To raise the money, we sold an organ bought a year before to encourage any musical talent hidden in our offspring. A year of lessons and sulking resulted in eight badly played bars of 'Little Donkey', and all four of us agreed that the instrument was superfluous to requirements.

We did the shop conversion ourselves, with the help of a friend, Ken Smith, who was a D.I.Y. enthusiast. We pulled out walls and plastered and rewired; we plumbed in new sinks and lavatories and decorated and tiled; we built a bar and made the tables and laid the floor; we leased the equipment and bought a sign which read 'Malynkis' – an amalgam of Malc and Lynne. (Wonder which genius thought of that.) I must say, inside it was pretty chic with its black, white and stainless steel decor, set off by a window full of red geraniums (pelargoniums.) Ah!

On our first day of trading we took £8.36, which delighted us, but a local health nut had eaten the geraniums and it cost £6 to replace them. We worked harder than we'd ever worked in our lives. We got up at 6 a.m. to start making bacon and tomato butties for the Co-op Bakery and homeward-bound shift workers. Then it was breakfasts from 8 to 10, coffees and snacks till noon, lunches till 3, tea and cakes till 5, then dinner and take-away until midnight.

I'd leave the shop at 6 p.m., drive off to a gig, (reeking of chips despite bathing nightly in Domestos) and return in time for the hour and a half of cleaning which began as soon as the last customer left at midnight.

Our takings went up by a few shillings each week and pretty soon we had to expand and move the kitchens upstairs, where Malc's Mom made our 'famous home-made pies'. One of our regulars would call three times a week for a take-away of: 'Ellomeyat pie and chips.'

'Why do you call it Ellomeyat pie?' we eventually asked.

''Cos if I find a bit of meat, I say to myself, "'ello – meyat!"'

Within a short time we had nine staff working full- and part-time. The business was successful, with potential to expand into outside catering, but the work had taken its toll. I had lost a stone in weight, which being thin in the first place I couldn't afford, and looked haggard and drawn. Malc was tired out, often giving me mornings in bed and coping with the work-load himself. We hardly saw the kids and when we did, we were nasty-tempered with them and each other. Living in two tiny rooms above the shop wasn't helping. We started house-hunting and found the perfect place on a new rural estate within ten minutes' drive of the café.

It was my dream house. A detached, three-bedroomed Georgian box with central heating, plastic columns and two pot lions on the step – six thousand quid, the lot.

Now that my wages were no longer required to subsidise the café, I scrimped and saved and redoubled my efforts on the clubs, saving the money for furniture and carpets. I sewed curtains and quilts and the boys were allowed to choose their own colour schemes and furnishings. I bought a long yearned for Gimson and Slater leather suite at an outrageous cost of £600 which I paid unfailingly each month over a year.

For a short time, life was bliss. I was a proper Mom at last, there when the kids came home from school with time to listen to them. I was a proper wife, ever ready with a hot bath and a soothing word for my weary provider. I revelled in the routine normality of wash-days and window-cleaning days and only accepted week-end club dates.

It was a short respite. The café started to founder. The bakery closed, the steel works went on short time. Shops were coming up for sale all over the precinct. We watched the area die in a matter of months. The rent still had to be paid and it was impossible to sell the lease with so much property available. Our expansion had necessitated the leasing of more expensive equipment and in a short time the café was losing a lot of money.

Clubs were cancelling mid-week bookings due to short time and I had to travel farther afield to find work. My earnings now had to pay the mortgage and household bills as well as subsidise the café.

Malc was still struggling to revive our ailing business, leaving me to travel alone and, despite my well-earned local reputation for purity – 'The only place Marti Caine performs is on stage' – I was prey to the occasional foreign wolf.

On one occasion I was breaking in new territory in Lincolnshire and my fellow 'artiste' – a male singer who shall remain nameless – moved in on me. Employing a lounge-lizard gait, he swaggered towards me as I stood at the bar waiting for my Coke. Leaning on the bar with one arm, he wrapped the other round my shoulder and said something like, 'Hi, babe. I'm Simon Place.'

'What's a nice Place like you doing in a boy like this?'

He laughed down his nose, trying to sound smooth, and a huge green plug of congealed snot landed with a 'thwap' on the back of my hand, which was resting on the bar. It must have been up there for years, it weighed at least 14 carats and sat like a throbbing lime fruit pastille on the back of my unmoving hand.

'Ahh! For me?' I asked, batting my eyelids.

He was mortified. With a Raleigh-esque flourish he threw a hanky over the unexploded missile and scraped it up, apologising profusely, before pocketing the prize and slinking off, red-faced and too embarrassed to talk to me for the rest of the evening.

Malc closed the shop eventually and we hit the road together once again, his Mother and Father moving in to take care of the boys while we toured from Land's End to John O'Groats in pursuit of sufficient money to pay off our debts. It was a hopeless task, we were slowly sinking in the mire.

Mr Green, the local bailiff, became a regular visitor, usually calling when Mother was in charge of the house. He was a delightful man. Soft and gentle with a quiet sense of humour, he got more money out of his debtors than any of his fellows. Mother liked him and began to look forward to his visits, and would greet him with: 'Hello, Mr Green. Come in and take a chair.'

'I've come for t'lot, Mrs Stringer!'

'Aye. Well, they're touring Scotland at the moment, they'll be back bi Wednesday.'

'O.K. I'll put this court order in the drawer with the others. Tell 'em they should get away with ten bob a week on this one.'

Things were looking grim. 'New Faces' didn't happen a moment too soon.

11

Christmas Day
University Arms Hotel

Two feet of silver Christmas tree, (stolen from the theatre), stands on top of the T.V. surrounded by cards. Crumpled wrapping paper froths out of a tightly packed waste-paper bin and two brightly painted Mexican cats – a gift from Kenneth – guard a neat array of unwrapped presents. A pair of ridiculous 'Miss Piggy' slippers from Lee, a pair of equally ridiculous 'Garfield' slippers from Max, a hand-knitted white cardigan from Carol, perfume, chocolates, bubble bath and frilly undies fill the hotel room with Christmas cheer.

Christmas in an hotel room isn't everyone's idea of bliss, but Kenneth's presence makes it home, and we spend the morning sitting in bed listening to a carol service on the radio, watching Walt Disney and nibbling on an assortment of Marks and Spencer goodies before the heat of the room rendered them inedible.

After bathing and dressing we wander down to the surprisingly well attended dining room for Christmas lunch. Three or four tables are surrounded by large happy families chatting, laughing and toasting each other's health. The rest are occupied by morose couples, mostly women, pairs of widowed sisters or spinster daughters with ageing mothers, and two Golden Wedding survivors who gaze out of a window across the green expanse of Parkers Piece, having run out of conversation years ago.

A small girl, acting on instructions from her parents, approaches the old couple's table and with a shy smile offers one end of a Christmas cracker to the old man, who snatches it from her grasp and stuffs it into his pocket.

'Pull the cracker with the little girl, dear,' coaxes the old woman.

'No. No. It's mine.' Then turning to the child, he snarls: 'Go away!'

The child steps back as if slapped, and a little gasp precipitates a trembling lower lip. The old woman reaches out to her, but the child turns and runs for the sanctuary of her mother's arms. The entire family is understandably shocked and hurt and the father, red-faced with rage, scrapes back his chair and despite his wife's restraining hand, strides towards the couple, napkin tucked in collar.

The old man blinks up through milky, uncomprehending eyes as the father, leaning over the table on knuckled hands, spits out his loathing in a voice too low to be overheard. He spins back to his family, snatching the napkin from his collar, his chin jutting righteously from beneath a press-lipped mouth.

Throughout, the old lady sits silent, hands on lap, eyes on agitated thumbs and as she looks up to witness the man's retreat her tear-streaked face is racked with pain.

The old man resumes his window gazing, a kindly smile lighting his face and his fragile fingers beating a soft tattoo on the table to accompany his humming. He smiles at his wife lovingly and she reaches across and pats his hand, loving him for what he was and not the stranger he has become.

Alzheimer's disease. The nurse suffers infinitely more than the patient. Old age doesn't seem to have much to offer, yet I desperately hope to attain it.

The little girl seems to have forgotten the incident and stops feeding her new doll to return my wave as we leave the dining room. The family are beginning to bubble again and we stop and chat happily to the old couple. But the whole incident has depressed me and for the first time since being diagnosed it occurs to me that I might be dying. (**You make me** sick. **You really do, you pile of self-pity. Read the letters, woman. Read the letters!**)

Since the news broke, I've received thousands of wonderful letters. The response has taken my breath away, I had no idea there were so many people who cared. Reading them lifts my spirits so much I feel I could conquer the world. I wish I could share these feelings with those who don't have a soul to care whether they live or die. (**That sounds really schmaltzy.**)

I hired a lovely secretary called Cats to help me cope with the mail, thinking at first of compiling a form letter, but they *all* merit a personal reply, so from 10 a.m. between shows until 10 p.m. I dictate and Cats scribbles away and bashes out the replies on the word processor kindly loaned to us by the theatre.

When I return to my hotel after the show, I open the new deliveries and read through them.

I've had letters offering encouragement, hope, love, prayers, advice, free holidays and Christmas dinners.

I've had letters from lords, ladies, bishops, priests, university dons, healers, herbalists, homeopathists and hypnotherapists.

I've had grape cures, pepper cures, mustard cures, self-cures, water cures, Swiss, African and Indian cures.

I've had bibles, books, St Christophers, holy water, rosaries, crosses, medallions, prayer cards, plants, hankies, heather, good luck charms, cuddly toys, a £7 postal order to start a fund and a £1 coin taped to the bottom of a letter signed simply 'an O.A.P.'

I've had phone calls and flowers from actors and actresses, models and dancers, directors and producers.

Bouquets arrive daily, one from Coronation Street's Lynne Perry – the best comedienne of her day and my idol and inspiration.

Jim Davidson sent six bottles of champagne with a card saying, 'What a way to get into the papers,' and one evening I received the largest basket of poinsettias I've ever seen, totally stunning, with a card saying, 'Thinking of you – lots of love, Elton.'

I've had funny letters, sad letters, letters from children, teenagers, young mums and grans, but mostly letters from fellow sufferers, relating their own experiences.

I don't stand a hope in hell of answering them all but I'm going to try my damnedest, and to that end have missed out on most of the company parties and outings. The permanent festive air of the Green Room helps lessen the fatigue of shorthand and dictation. My dressing room is tiny – six feet square – and Cats has to sit on the floor of the Green Room propped against my open door, writing furiously while coping with the pranks of the dwarfs.

The little people are delightful and great fun and while there is no separatism in the company, there is an impenetrably close bond between the dwarfs. They seem able to communicate with each other without words and are extremely sensitive to atmosphere. There is a mystic, psychic quality about them that is pleasantly disturbing, and often one of them will gently take my hand and gaze steadily into my eyes as if willing me better and I feel sort of honoured to be welcomed into their society.

Paul Scot Harris, who plays Catsmeat, my familiar, leaps off stage and runs across the seat-backs, zig-zagging his way to the rear of the auditorium and back, leaping over the heads of squealing delighted children and the ducking ones of parents. It's a spectacular scene and I make a point of leaving my dictation and watching through the curtains each evening. He's the ex-professional Latin American dance champion and, if he slipped, could break a leg and ruin his career. I forget to breathe out every time I watch him. If you want to thrill an audience, taking risks is essential. I did it myself to earn stardom.

In 1972, when the café was in its infancy, I acquired a new agent. His name was Johnnie Peller. Due to his reputation for honesty, he was fast becoming the top agent in Yorkshire, sole booker of at least sixty clubs, and had fifty or more acts signed to him.

He approached me in the Limes Club in Sheffield and said if

I signed with him, he would fill my book and raise my fee – a promise which he fulfilled.

Poeple with artistic temperaments are rarely practical with money and are easy to rip-off. John's manner was off-putting to the faint-hearted, but as I slowly got to know him, realised his lack of physical and social grace covered an ultra-soft centre, and I came to love the man.

He is one of life's rare characters: rotund and balding, with semitic features and all the vernacular. (My life already!) He conducted business round a large, rarely lit cigar clamped permanently between his lips (those in the know said he slept with it) and was like a caricature of Mr Ten Percent with shrugging shoulders and upward-facing palms.

He was fastidious about his hair, which he grew long and lacquered in place over a balding pate. Once, on a tour of the Middle East, the gentlemen of the orchestra were watching him swim – cigar in place – up and down the hotel pool. His hair was trailing behind him like a veil and Mike, the bass, observed that he looked as though he was trawling for mackerel; and as he turned, Colin, the drummer, said: 'Bugger me! He's caught one.'

John has great courage. As a young man he was cursed with a dreadful stammer, and to help combat it he became a club singer, not easy under the best of circumstances. He succeeded and was left with just a slight hesitation in speech. Then he became an agent.

In November 1974, it was he who talked me into going along for the audition for 'New Faces' at the Blue Angel night-club in Leeds. I didn't want to go. It was pointless, I had no ambition to become a 'star'. Showbiz was a means to an end. I remained in it only to pay off the debts left by our now failed business and needed every penny I could get.

I certainly couldn't afford to waste petrol chasing rainbows as far as Leeds and back. Besides, I cleaned the windows on

Fridays, so I didn't have time.

John said it wouldn't cost much in petrol as Pat McClusky, an excellent comic, was driving a minibus over with eight of John's other acts and I could go with them. Julie Rose would be there and would return the yellow shoes I'd left in a dressing room two weeks ago. It would be fun, and what had I got to lose? So I went.

The place was heaving when we arrived; there must have been a thousand people squashed into the confines of the Blue Angel club, all waiting to do three minutes for Les Cox and his production team, sitting invisibly beyond the strong footlights on the small stage.

I sat with one eye on the clock, waiting my turn and listening to the twenty-fifth rendering of 'My Way'. If they didn't get a move on, I would miss my gig and lose vital cash – as I hadn't come in my own car, I was stranded. I was about to accept a lift home from B.B. and John, a double act who were working Sheffield that night, when my name was called.

I went on and delivered a fast three minutes of the cleanest material I had, most of which had been done to death already by every comic who went before me and would no doubt be done again by those who followed. I didn't care – time was of the essence and I was eager to get home, sort out the kids and get to my gig.

I promptly forgot about the audition, considering it a waste of time, so was astounded when John phoned four days later to say I had passed the audition and would be hearing from Les Cox when he'd decided which show I'd be on.

Luck plays a great part in success and as mine would have it, I was chosen for the pre-Christmas show. By chance, the comic who was booked had changed his show for a later one as he was in pantomime. The show also had a majority of male acts so a female comic was perfect. I was only given a few days' notice. I wished for a new dress as I washed and ironed my old yellow home-made mini for the hundredth time.

Home-made mini or not, I won the show. Luck again. My opening line, shouted to an imaginary stage-hand in the wings, was supposed to be: 'Will you switch these fans off, please? I'm getting sucked up.'

Nerves got the better of me and only when Les Cox stopped me to go for another take did I realise I'd got my letters mixed up and had inadvertently said: 'Will you switch these sans off please? I'm getting . . .' and so on.

The audience loved it. I ad-libbed for a few minutes while the re-take was set up and they warmed to me, which boosted my confidence and gave me the edge. Ted Ray, one of the judges, reminded me that I now had to work out an act for 'The All Winners Show', which happened every seventh week, a contest between the six previous show winners. This was the sixth show, so I had six days to work out a new act.

Inspiration hit me like a bolt from the blue on the way home. I had six days – time to make myself an evening gown (evening gowns aren't funny) that drops to pieces (how?) after I've fallen down a flight of stairs. (You'll break your neck.) To hell with the risk, I had three minutes to create an impact (being carried off on a stretcher should do it).

I bought some black jersey scalloped with gold embroidery from the market, and made a long, three-tiered, halter-necked gown. The first tier finished at mini-length, the second at my knees and the third at my ankles. Each tier was held in place by tiny press studs which sprang apart at the least pressure.

I had bought an Afro wig and added hooks on to a charm bracelet, then worked out three minutes of self-deprecating material which I wrapped up in a song – Roberta Flack's 'Killing Me Softly'. At rehearsals, Les Cox agreed it would be wiser not to practise falling down the stairs as it was a skill which took months to acquire – better just to go for it on the night.

It was my turn. I was last on, in case the fall went wrong. I stood looking down a flight of seven stairs in my Afro wig, custom-built frock and charm bracelet, listening to the band tune up and waiting for my intro.

The stairs were just right, I was confident the act would work, the song was one of my best, but something was wrong. THE AUDIENCE – they didn't recognise me. Some sixth sense prompted me to remove my wig, revealing my outrageous but identifiable orange hair, and I waved and shouted, 'It's me. It's me!' before jamming the wig back on.

It worked. An excited buzz went through the audience, they giggled conspiratorially and settled back to wait with an air of expectancy.

They weren't disappointed. I was announced, the orchestra struck up and the intro of 'Killing Me Softly' filled the studio. I sang the first sixteen bars in a soft velvet voice, standing perfectly still and letting the sad lyrics speak for themselves. On the first note of the following eight-bar break I took the first step, missed the second and somersaulted down the rest, orchestrated by drum rolls and cymbal crashes as the rest of the band dissolved into discord.

The audience rose as one and a shocked intake of breath hung in silence for a second, before they broke into hysterical laughter.

My wig was swinging from the hooks on the charm bracelet, my orange hair tumbled over my face like a pound of grapes in an egg-cup and one shoe-less leg stuck out of a semi-detached dress. I hobbled over to collect the missing shoe and the dress detached itself a press stud at a time, disengaging itself completely as I bent – bottom to camera – to retrieve the shoe.

I won, which put me in the final contest between all the winners of the 'All Winners' contest which was to be televised, live, from the London Palladium in July.

The second I walked off the set, a wave of pain hit me and I looked down at my grazed shins and one swollen knee. The bruises lasted for months, but it was well worth it.

John was like a new father, handing out cigars and strutting around like chief turkey in the yard. He worked out a new management contract with a sliding scale rate of commission, starting at 10 per cent on £100 per week, up to 25 per cent over £499 per week. FOUR HUNDRED AND NINETY-NINE POUNDS – impossible.

Within weeks I was paying 25 per cent commission.

Along with the bruises, I was left with the problem of what to do in the Grand Final, and eventually came up with the idea of a prop stool which would collapse at the touch of a button and jump up again on its own.

A firm in Maidenhead designed an hydraulically operated bar stool with a large base housing a compressed air tank. The stool was built into the set and was triggered by pressing down on the foot-rest. John and Malc watched hours of rehearsals from the stalls of the Palladium, both becoming more nervous by the second. The stool was complicated and, I felt, rather contrived. Simple slapstick is always best.

The competition was strong. An exciting group called 'O Fanchi', an original impressionist called Aidan J. Harvey and some excellent singers. But my three biggest problems were a Liverpudlian comic, Al Dean, a young black impressionist, Lenny Henry and a uniquely funny singer/songwriter named Victoria Wood.

I tried to tell myself it didn't matter. Offers were pouring in, my money was increasing by the week and I'd already signed with A.T.V. for a T.V. show with five other 'New Faces' acts – Victoria Wood and Lenny Henry among them.

I was last on. The Palladium was packed. You only got one

shot – this was live television – and I stood in the wings, rigid with fear, listening to my heart booming. I had on a white guipure lace dress and matching turban with a huge feather on the front. I took my place at the top of a walkway between the orchestra, the curtains opened and a lush sigh from the string section led the intro of 'Memories'. Voice trembling slightly, I sang the first chorus, mouth too near the mike, and glided towards the stool.

Then I slid on to the stool and began the second verse, seated, then hit the foot-rest and the stool began a too-slow descent which fortunately gathered enough momentum to throw me off. It was supposed to shoot back up again, hitting my jutting backside en route and pitching me across the stage, but it didn't. I scrambled to my feet, forcing the turban over my eyes and bending the feather till it stuck out like a pan-handle, went nervously into the comedy routine and finished by singing, 'If There's a Wrong Way to Do It' and walking into the proscenium arch.

I was disappointed with my performance. I'd blown it, and I stood on stage in a semi-circle with the rest of the acts and an artificially bright smile, while the compère read out the marks awarded to each act by the three judges.

The results are greeted by wild applause as one act is toppled from the lead by another and so on. Only four results left and so far Lenny Henry has just taken a clear lead from Victoria Wood. It looks as though he's won, but no, the Liverpudlian comic, Al Dean, is awarded 97 out of a possible 100 points.

He's won. I thought he would, he deserves it and suddenly the semi-circle is clapping and looking at me: 'She's won, she's a-a-a won,' I hear John shout from half-way up the stalls, and my fellow contestants are slapping me on the back and pushing me to the front of the stage,

'.. so with ninety-eight points, Marti Caine is the outright *winner of New Faces 1975' and Cinderella went to the ball.*

*My experience at the Fiesta Club had led me to the con-
clusion that, on average, a 'star' lasts about three years before
fading to a nonentity and I intended to earn as much as possible
in that time and retire – unhurt – with enough capital for a business.*

*Some of the big London agencies were circling like bees
round honey and a few had actually offered to 'buy' me from
John. They tried to attract me by offering tempting morsels – one
offered me a Rolls-Royce with a personalised number plate – but
my loyalties belonged to John. I couldn't kick him in the teeth
after three years of good work and live with myself. Besides, he
believed in me, so we remained a team for another decade.*

The press are *still* hanging around in dribs and drabs and
I feel safer confined to my room when not at the theatre.
The letters are manna from heaven, filling my time and
recharging my batteries.

Max rang to wish me a merry one, followed by Lee
and my sister-in-law, Maureen, and while Kenneth
snoozed beside me I rang my 'lot', culminating in a long
chat with my lovely ex mom-in-law.

Christmas Day 1988 has been delightful if unre-
markable and we snuggle down after pigging out on
room service and a floor picnic of the remaining Marks
and Spencer goodies.

More marble-sized lumps have sprung up on my
neck and in my right armpit and the lump on my thigh is
growing fast. As I float on the surface of sleep, I put my
Knights to work.

They're disenchanted. I've changed the mental
image of the cancer from the multi-headed dragon to
football-sized balloons full of water – unfortunately there

are millions of them, all over, some clustered into piles beneath the lumps on my body. My Knights plod around spiking them with their lances, but it's such boring work and they're beginning to feel defeated by sheer numbers. It's a hopeless task. I'll have to change the image of the cancer again.

Monday 26 December

The entire cast, in costume and make-up, sets off in a vintage bus at 10 a.m. on the traditional annual pilgrimage to the children's hospital. Laden with presents, we surge through wide modern corridors, glossy-floored and walled with nursery transfers, children's art work and Christmas decorations. Balloons nose the corners of a toy-scattered communal area where recuperating, dressing-gowned children dart around the legs of nurses, mums and dads, in pursuit of a Tonka truck or balsawood plane.

A boisterous little boy, robbed of hair and eyebrows by a cruel chemotherapy, says, 'Hello. Why are you wearing that funny hat?'

'Knock, Knock.'

'Who's there?'

'Scot.'

'Scot who?'

'Scot nothing to do with you!' A husky laugh and he runs off to try out the gag on a wheel-chaired pallid little pal, recovering from a recent kidney transplant. I watch as laughter paints his thin sallow face with a flash of rosy health and his 'old man' eyes become an 8-year-old's again.

The side wards hold heartbreak. Kids too sick to raise their heads, lying soft and limp beneath the burden of heart disease, kidney failure and cancers that eat everything but innocence. They haven't even begun to live and they're dying.

A young vicar and his wife, with matching haunted faces, wheel their beautiful chubby little daughter down the corridor. They are waiting for a kidney donor and time is running out fast; I wonder if his faith has been weakened or strengthened.

'This is Cathy.' A sleeping porcelain doll wired up to an intravenous drip. 'She's having chemotherapy for leukaemia.' Her eyelids yawn to expose vivid blue eyes and a life force shining like a beacon.

'She'll be O.K.'

In the last ward, an 8-year-old girl rejecting a kidney transplant. Her chances are slim. I sit beside her mum, who grasps my arm with both hands, like a drowning woman. She regards me with the same bright smile as her child's, but tears are rolling down her face and her eyes say, 'I'm losing her.'

The child's smile never wavers though her eyes are knowing. Her courage is enormous. It lends itself to me and I return to the theatre strangely renewed.

12

New Year's Eve 1988

It's been a busy week: a 21st party for Dawn the dancer, a theatre party where the cast *thrashed* the crew at charades, dinner with the gentlemen of the orchestra at Browns, a charity dinner and a silly supper with the principals where we all did a party piece.

I did my usual bird impression – 'A Vulture' – best executed in Valentino or Yves St Laurent, with knees tucked under armpits, toes clawed over the edge of a sturdy table and neck and mouth stretched to capacity until the cords and sinews stand out. With one eye closed, you peer miserably round the room and say, 'Patience be damned, I'm gonna *kill* something.' (Try it! It goes down a treat at family do's.)

The cast and crew get on famously and are throwing yet another party – a 'vicars and tarts' one I believe (you're made for it), but I decline this evening's invitation out of reverence for my Mom.

The phone is ringing as I fumble with the key, my bladder is bursting and as I fall into the room I'm undecided which call to answer first. The phone wins and I'm so glad; it's Rog, calling from some distant port.

Roger Carr has been my close friend and musical director for the past fourteen years, and, until my marriage to Kenneth in 1985, shared my life and my flat in Sheffield.

After winning 'New Faces', the first thing I needed was a musical director. Venues boasting 'Fred ont' thorgan' and 'Bert ont' drums' were getting rarer and I found myself working more and more with small orchestras. With the help of John, Malc and I auditioned several excellent musicians, none of which became one with me. I knew it was possible. It had happened on rare occasions in the past. Working with a different pianist each night provided an infinite variety of the best and worst musicians in the country, and among the best were the few who listened with a different ear, who could lose the rest of the world and let voice and instrument be controlled by a joint spirit.

The prize for winning 'New Faces' was a trip to Las Vegas and a three-week cabaret stint at the M.G.M. Grand, where I died four times nightly during each 45-minute spot. Malc and Johnnie Peller accompanied me, along with a journalist and photographer from TV Times.

John had hired a press agent called Clifford Elson (clever John – a good press agent is essential to a showbiz career and Clifford is the best). He set up the TV Times coverage, and we all pretended to be having a wonderful time for the benefit of the camera. I was shoved into dressing rooms throughout Vegas to stand beside some bemused star for a photograph and Glen Campbell, Lovelace Watkins and Liberace stood and grinned like old pals. When we returned home, the search for a musical director became a priority.

It was 3 o'clock in the afternoon when Malc pulled open the fire doors, left ajar on Sundays, at the back of the Aquarius Club in Chesterfield. The smell of stale beer and cigarette smoke spilled into the back-stage corridors as we groped along in search of my dressing room. We were early for band call and, except for a gap-toothed, long-haired hippie groping along in the opposite direction, seemed to be alone. The sound began before our search was completed and it stopped me in my tracks, leaving Malc to continue alone. The soft, sweet sounds of the piano dropped round me, intoxicating me and compelling me to follow as I drifted towards the sound like a child of Hamelin. It was the hippie. He smiled absently on catching sight of me, and I wandered over and stood in the well of the Steinway. He carried on playing.

'Hello, Marti.' His voice was soft and without accent. 'Congratulations on winning "New Faces". You deserved it. Think you should have done more singing, though.' And he started playing through some of the songs from my club repertoire, answering my enquiring look with, 'I worked with you a couple of years back, in East Dean Working Men's Club.' I began to hum and before I knew it, a tidal wave of crystal-clear sound swept my voice to hitherto undiscovered heights and depths, racing through tunnels of octaves until the sound wasn't my own and my ears heard a stranger singing. It was wonderful, he felt it too; I had found my musical director.

He was 24, highly intelligent, could drink Malc under the table and had a dry, lightning wit. Though he only lived five miles away from 'Tanglewood' – our newly acquired house – it was often more convenient, when we were rehearsing, for him to stay in the guest room. Each visit guaranteed he would leave behind some of his property and after a few weeks we'd accumulated his record player, eight boxes of books and his Rupert

Bear hot-water bottle. So it was no surprise to find he had moved in. The kids were going through the practical joke stage and, having exhausted their repertoire on us, were delighted to have a new victim. Roger, however had a few tricks of his own to counter with and a long hot summer season in Yarmouth was turned into 'The Wacky Races'. The house was full of kids and dogs, dancers and comics, spur-of-the-moment parties and welcome but unexpected visitors.

Most of the unexpected visitors were passing girl-friends of Roger's, so I was surprised when he informed me of the pending arrival of a very special girl-friend. She was French, her name was Joanne and she was from a well-respected French circus family. Roger usually introduced us to his girl-friends across the breakfast table, so this one had to be important and in the two weeks before her arrival I asked Rog to teach me a formal French greeting. Accommodatingly, he recorded a short speech for me to learn phonetically. I practised every day, Sony headset working overtime, and on her arrival delivered my welcome speech with ease and confidence before tearing off to prepare coffee and croissants.

Some weeks later, discussing the arts, she admitted the English sense of humour was difficult to understand initially, and only now could she laugh at my greeting of, 'Help, I am being bitten by a sanitary towel!'

When I gave up cabaret, Roger became musical director on board the *Canberra*. He loves it but his shore leave is brief and rare. He did some brilliant arrangements for me. The moment he touched the keys, we'd lose the world. Without him, I am deprived.

Wednesday 11 January 1989

Mail continues to pour in much faster than Cats and I can answer it, and among last week's was a book from lovely Katie Boyle and a letter saying, 'You're not dying, Marti, read this book.' It was by an oncologist called O.Carl Simmonton and entitled *Getting Well Again*.

It's fascinating and deals with attitude and mind control, using a technique called 'visualisation' which is more or less what I have been doing with my Knights.

The book has taught me where my imagery was wrong. I've replaced my Knights, and now employ my white blood cells in the shape of Royal Marine beavers, who joyously seek out the cancer cells – now fish-eggs – and devour them with relish. It feels right. Although the book suggests my beavers should be aggressive, alas, try as I might, I can't get them to be anything less than over-joyed at the prospect of more delicious fish-eggs.

Malc and his wife Lynda came to see the show last Saturday. And Lee and his girl-friend, Suzanne, drove up from Plymouth in time to miss it, but joined us for dinner at Browns. They all stayed over and we had a superb Sunday lunch at the Garden House Hotel, lazing around until late afternoon when we went our separate ways.

Lynda was a little tired. She's had a hectic Christmas – one long round of shopping, cleaning and cooking for the entire family, including Malc's brother and his wife and his mother, who has become confused and forgetful since Dad's death and Lynda has taken care of her with selfless dedication.

She married into the worst of Mother's years, whereas I had the best, and I wonder if I'd have been as unselfish as Lynda.

Providence saw fit to favour me with wonderful in-laws. They eagerly embraced me into a family rich with eccentric aunts, brainy brothers, cranky grannies and caustic uncles, and the day they began referring to me as 'our Lynne' was the happiest day of my life.

I belonged to someone.

I was hungry for the security of routine and revelled in roast beef Sundays and meat-pie Mondays. I loved the rituals of housewifery passed from mother to daughter, which remained untarnished by a young commercial television. No 'Rael-Brook shirt with the London look' ever drip-dried on the line of this household; shirts were boiled, ponshed, dolly-blued, mangled and starched. No one ever looked 'a little lovelier each day with fabulous new Camay' – a bar of green Fairy soap worked as well on faces as it did on floors.

It was bliss shopping for 'a nice bit of haslet for father's packing-up' and knowing for certain that thirty-six milk checks – no more, no less – would be required each week.

I still warm myself on memories of family parties where Uncle Brian would sing 'Unchained Melody' into a glass, Aunty Rosy would become more argumentative after her third sherry, Uncle Harold would lecture on the brilliance of Enoch Powell, and Dad would lead us in a community rendering of:

> *'My brother, Sylvest,'*
> *(What has he got)*
> *'He's got a row of forty medals on his chest'*
> *(Big Chest).*

Dad was a shy man, who wore the trousers and covered his soft centre with a brusque manner and the stern countenance of a bloodhound. He would glower at me over his jowls and tease with expressions like, 'Thinks she's china and she's pot-mould,' *or, 'Thinks she's a race-horse and she's a pit-pony.'* Compliments didn't trip off his tongue too easily and *'You'll do'* was the height of praise. His accent was Yorkshire, bordering on Barnsley, and his *'wuckin' boyits'* were Cherry Blossomed to gleaming perfection each evening and placed under the *'stoyil'* he sat on.

He was a file-grinder by trade, sitting astride a roaring belt-driven stone wheel, breathing in dust for eight hours a day until chronic bronchitis and pneumoconiosis drove him to an early retirement. Any exertion would result in long coughing bouts and Mother never complained about the hours of sleep lost each night as she ran up and down stairs with bowls of steaming inhalants, aspirators and balsams in an attempt to ease his suffocating agony.

Each morning he would rise and make the fire to warm the house and, when the rest of the family came downstairs, we would find him in his armchair, elbows propped on spread knees and braces straining against vested shoulders as they heaved with suppressed coughing. Like all long-term coughers he had developed a noise-reducing technique, and all that could be heard was a chuck-chuck-chuck sound that would go on for long minutes at a time, gradually winding down like a clockwork drummer until every scrap of air was squeezed out of his poor concrete lungs. Eyes bulging from a purple, blue-lipped face, he would at last draw in a tortuous gasp of air and the whole process would begin again.

Mother took everything in her stride, a kind, consistently calm woman whose family was everything. Thanks to her capable care – and much to the surprise of the doctors – he didn't succumb until the age of seventy, despite his daily 'only bit a pleasure', ten Woodbines and a box of Swans.

One of his red-letter days was the time we took him for his first ride in our newly acquired Rolls-Royce. He tried not to look impressed as he slid gingerly across the cream leather of the *front seat.*

'Is these seats genuine vinyl, then, our Malc?'

Malc clicked Dad's seat-belt in place, lowered his arm-rest and rocked silently away from the house that had always been home. We wound sedately along the narrow, grass-verged roads of 'The Oval' council estate and glided through the town centre and five miles beyond, before reaching Ringinglow Road – long, isolated and Roman straight – and putting the car through its paces.

Dad gazed with stony-faced approval at the walnut dash, jewelled with clocks and dials. He tentatively twisted the chrome swivel-ball air-conditioning vent so that it pointed in his direction. He had mistaken it for an ashtray and I watched from the back seat as he painstakingly flicked his ash on to the small pile of dead matches and cigarette ends that he'd accumulated in the bowl of the vent. With all the enthusiasm of a second-hand car dealer, Malc was extolling the virtues of the car, pushing buttons and levers as he drove. Dad leapt with alarm as, at the touch of a button, the passenger window slid down taking his chin-supporting arm with it; and when his seat position was electronically altered, we were rewarded with a cry of 'What the bloody 'ell . . . ?!'

' . . . it's a wonderful piece of engineering, Dad . . .' continued Malc, '. . . it virtually drives itself. It tells you when there's ice on the road. I can set this cruise control to any speed I want and it drives without me having to touch the accelerator. It checks its own oil, checks its own petrol and watch this . . .' and he flicked on the high-powered air-conditioning. An icy blast of air hit Dad full in the face, taking with it the matches, ash and fag-ends and strewing them over his head and chest.

'Bugger me,' he said. 'It even empties its own ashtrays!'

Friday 13 January

What a day! After a pleasant lunch with Mr Blackwood, the managing director of the Cambridge Arts Theatre, I joined the rest of the cast in the Green Room to help write a Derek and Clive type 'blue' review to be performed for the benefit of our admirable crew after tonight's show. It's traditional at the Cambridge Arts and our review is given extra impetus by an equally blue send-up of the pantomime, performed for our benefit by the crew.

The crew panto began at 11 p.m. with thunder and lightning and a large hairy flyman wearing my Red Queen dress, crown and high heels. He parodied my groping stumble across the stage to the podium and gathered up the skirt to reveal hairy legs and bloomers. Wobbling his way up the steps, he lifted his arms to a descending mirror and commanded:

> 'Mirror, Mirror on the wall
> Who is the fairest of them all?'
> 'Snow White,' said the mirror.

'No shit!?' lisped the flyman, hand on camp hip, and so it went on. The Forest Deer had more than just the antlers sticking out of his costume, the animal ballet was just that and an X-rated version of 'Hi-Ho' was rendered by seven stage-hands with boots on their knees.

It was hilarious and much appreciated by the select audience of usherettes, theatre staff and cast. Our own show followed – a send-up of 'New Faces' with six acts and a foul-mouthed panel – and was equally appreciated.

It was 2 a.m. by the time I joined Kenneth Cranham and his wife, Fiona Victory, in the lounge of the University Arms Hotel. They had come to see the show and my guilt for neglecting them afterwards was eased by Pam and Kath, also at the show this evening, who entertained them in my absence.

Sometimes I don't know whether I'm playing Pam or Pam's playing me – we're so alike. I suppose it comes from being lifelong buddies – you rub off on each other, reflect each other's personality. I'm so lucky to have her.

Monday 16 January – 4 a.m.
The Cottage

The suitcases stand in the hallway, repacked with clothes I've spent all night washing and pressing.

We drove home yesterday in a car tightly packed with the contents of the dressing room, two sacks of mail and the accumulated clobber of a six-week season.

Saturday night's last performance was followed by a frantic 'get out' to make way for the next show, tear-filled goodbyes and promises to write daily. I enjoyed the show immensely and will miss them all.

I can hear Kenneth running his bath. We leave for the airport at 6 a.m. His briefcase bulges on the table, full of slides and biopsy reports, medical histories and letters from Dr McKenzie and Professor Sikora, as well as his own carefully compiled notes. If it hadn't been for his diligent research and dogged answer seeking, I wouldn't be leaving for America two hours from now in the hope of a cure. I think God sent Kenneth.

13

Thursday 19 January

A Farrah Fawcett blow-up doll with stuck-on smile breezed towards us as we stepped through parting plate-glass into the cool marbled elegance of the downtown Palo Alto 'Surgicentre', one of a plethora of 'fast-food' medical practices surrounding Stanford University Hospital.

'Hi there, welcome to Surgicentre.' She said like a game-show host, and before we could reply, continued: 'My name's Candy. I'm your reception nurse. You must be Lynne Ives. If you could fill in our form and a cheque for the amount stated on the attached invoice, we can get started. Mr Ives, would you care to take a seat?' And her white Reboks screeched at the marble as she turned and led me to the waiting forms. She looked as good from the back as she did from the front and Kenneth's Exorcet missile eyes homed in on her pink, uniformed rump and stayed there.

Having taken care of the business (**an American priority**) she flashed the teeth in Kenneth's direction once more and said: 'Lynne's surgery will take about ninety minutes. She'll be all prettied up and ready to go two hours from now. If you'd care to stay, there's coffee and magazines over there, or you could call back to collect her at noon.'

'I'll call back at noon,' he said to the buttons on her breast pockets, and she led me to a changing room full of paper nighties before turning to greet the next chicken on the conveyor belt and rewinding the tape to: 'Hi there, welcome to Surgicentre. My name's Candy, I'm your . . .'

It was obviously a very successful practice, providing instant vascular and general surgery on an outpatient level. It boasted a team of five surgeons – Doctors Slachman, Eisenstat, Bloodnott, Nudleman and Smith (**Smith must be a foreigner**).

I'd met Dr Eisenstat yesterday. He confirmed that the lump on my thigh was indeed big enough for a biopsy and that Dr Slachman would be performing the small operation (**thank God it's not Bloodnott**).

I climbed into my paper nightie and was helped on to a narrow trolley by a second Farrah Fawcett blow-up doll (**but punctured**), then gazed adoringly up the nose of a Greek god as he wheeled me into an open lift and down to the basement operating theatre to a waiting: 'Hi, I'm Andy, your anaesthesiologist.'

Andy, my anaesthesiologist, gave me a smile and a pre-med jab and left me to float in a warm sea-green calm which was interrupted by the slap of rubber swing-doors and a breathless, 'Hi, my name's Nudleman. Slachman's stuck in traffic, but I can just about fit you in.

Andy! Go to work.' **(Shampoo this one while I comb out Mrs Brown.)** And Andy obligingly held a hissing white mask over my lower face.

I came to in a dentist-type chair, surrounded by Charlie's Angels – a pink one, a blue one and a green one. The green one asked if I'd like a vomit bowl. I declined. The pink one gave me a bottle of painkillers and the blue one asked if I needed my hair or make-up re-touched. Pink and blue drifted away, leaving green to chat for a few minutes – 'I jest lerved those cute red heels and hose you 'rived in' – before escorting me back to the changing room on the floor above.

I felt fine – refreshed almost – my leg a little sore but not enough to impede me, although I did wonder at the wisdom of the 'cute red heels and hose' as I wriggled my feet into the 4-inch-high stilettos. I was impressed by the streamlined efficiency of the Surgicentre **(if a little dismayed by the check 'em in, chop it off, chuck 'em out attitude)**. With the slightest of limps I walked to reception to find Kenneth waiting, and after saying goodbye to Candy, we joined José, waiting behind the wheel of the hotel limo.

José was a porter-cum-chauffeur at the delightful Stanford Park Hotel where we were staying and, like most of the staff, was working his way through college **(you could order your breakfast in Latin)..)** He was a second-year dental student with film-star looks, a superb physique, dark seductive eyes **(and a wife and two kids)**. He pointed out several good restaurants as we passed the magnificent Stanford shopping precinct.

We had arrived in San Francisco on Monday, after what seemed like an extremely long flight. We flew economy – I may have to make this trip regularly if

Stanford accept me, and my insurance doesn't cover me, so every penny counts. We're both prepared to sell everything we own (and busk cinema queues) should it become necessary, but I miss the leg-room of first class. (How quickly you've become blasé. Up to winning 'New Faces', you'd only been as far as the Isle of Man and considered yourself well-travelled.)

British Airways staff are *fantastic,* whatever class you travel, and plied Kenneth with enough booze to soften the effect of two *Sun* journalists who approached us for a story and picture after we'd been airborne for about eight hours. God knows how far they're prepared to pursue us or when it's going to stop. I felt so trapped, belted into my window seat with my knees tucked under my chin, and was terrified Kenneth would hit the photographer. They were very polite, however, and didn't take much persuading to go away.

A long wheel-based Lincoln lounged at the kerb outside San Francisco airport, its inner mystery guarded by tinted glass and a lady driver who smiled, 'Mr & Mrs Ives?' and strode forward, forcefully relieving Kenneth of our luggage. Bags booted, she opened the rear door on an area the size of your average lounge and bowed us inside. The door closed behind us with a satisfying 'thunk'.

The car rocked to a standstill in the walled and cobbled courtyard, outside the modern red-brick Stanford Park Hotel. A square of nine giant palm trees, close-planted in three rows of three, centred the yard and provided a shady canopy of fronds against a weak but bright sun. José, the handsome porter, stepped out to greet us and filled the courtyard with his dazzling smile. Pushing a renegade curl from his forehead, he divested the boot of our luggage and led the way to reception, where we said goodbye to Sandy, the lady driver.

The focal point of reception was a huge brick fireplace. The three upper floors had been peeled away allowing the chimney breast to rise, unhindered, to the roof. Kenneth checked in and, conscious of several pairs of curious eyes, I posed by the fireplace trying to look haughty and English and thinking how good my sombrero and black rubber raincoat looked against the red brick. I allowed my eyes to travel slowly up the length of the chimney breast, tilting my head back to take in the upper reaches, and my hat fell off. In an attempt to retrieve it gracefully, I did a half turn; the backs of my knees hit the arm of one of a pair of chairs and I toppled backwards over the chair and landed on my hat, wedged between the chairs with my legs in the air. All this happened in the twinkling of an eye and just as quickly I extricated myself from the upholstered prison, scraped up my hat and tried to bash it back into shape as I hobbled to retrieve a far-flung shoe.

Kenneth impressed them where I had failed, and our room was upgraded to a suite as soon as he laid the lardy accent on them.

The suite was superb: two bathrooms, kitchenette and bar, lounge, dining area and bedroom. The bed was comfortable and so large you had to shout sweet nothings.

We settled down to nine channels of T.V. and a tour of the room-service menu, ordering things we'd only read about – pastrami on rye; blue-jack cheese; sourdough bread and grits and black-eyed beans.

After a bath and an early night to stave off jet-lag, we awoke refreshed and ready for the mammoth breakfast of fresh berries and juice, buttered muffins, hash browns, bacon and eggs – sunny side up, of course – coffee for me and English breakfast tea for Kenneth. I was champing at the bit to investigate Stanford shopping precinct before my 2 p.m. hospital appointment with Dr Levy and his team, so Kenneth hastily finished his third helping and we walked the short distance to the precinct.

Panic! The shops didn't open until 10 and it was only 9.30. I wandered round the spectacular mall, deserted except for a few armed security guards, paint-smart in peaked hats and short-sleeved shirts. It was vast. Burnt brick paving wound round islands of rock gardens, fountains and mature trees, baubled with multicoloured hanging baskets peeking through their pea-green wisteria like leaves. Graceful glass arches and rose-clad pergolas led to secret places and yet another array of shops. Goods of every description beckoned like the fruits of Tantalus behind sparkling glass. I wished Pam was here.

At last the shops opened and like a kid with a tanner, I hunted and sniffed and tasted and tried, imagining what I'd buy if I had all the money in the world. The troves were many. A gallery selling imported Mexican and Asian art, hung with turquoise-creased bronzes and thongs of pewter bells, and piled with rope-fringed rugs and earth-hued shawls with a hint of dust and distant camels beneath the patchouli. Maceys, with a Beryl Cook character behind every counter: the big-breasted, blue-rinse with dropped eyelids and fat lips; the fish-nets and sling-backs with tight belt and red nails and the twinkly-eyed twin-set with home perm and beads. I skulked around the rails of haute couture feeling guilty for finger-ing fabric and scrutinising seams, but it's a habit I can't break.

I ran out of wrist in a perfume store, so sat and

sipped coffee outside a brasserie and watched a team of artists paint a *trompe l'oeil* scene on an adjacent wall. I'd seen two wonderful prints earlier: an American artist called Carol Grigg, not expensive, but I mustn't be tempted. (**Go on. Sod the expense – give the cat a gold-fish.**) Besides, they're framed – four by two and a half – I'll never get them home. (**Wanna bet?**) It's out of the question.

A shadow fell across my sunny table and I looked up to find Kenneth who'd been on a recce of the hospital, so after a lunch of ribs, skins, wings and blueberry pie, he was able to lead me through the appropriate doors of the vast, multi-entranced building.

Stanford University Hospital is the Hippocratic show-piece of America, whose government-sponsored research surges forward free of the confines of budget. A Champs Elysée corridor led us to an escalator and the plush basement waiting room of the cancer clinic. An apricot cave of pastel carpet and toning walls, soft lights, Mozart and easy chairs gave it a 'late evening lounge' feel, at odds with a white-capped staff bristling with efficiency behind the computerised reception.

Kenneth handed a letter of introduction to a reception nurse.

'Oh! You're the people from England.' And she keyed the proffered information into a machine which spat out a plastic 'membership' card bearing my name, rank and serial number. She asked us to take a seat until called and while Kenneth readied the contents of his briefcase, I studied fellow patients, fabricating their life stories.

There was the born-rich drug addict and his anguished girl-friend, identically clad in black tights, boots and jackets. They clung to each other, speaking in desperate whispers, sharing the shock and terror of a recently confirmed test result.

A much-loved mother, dimpled and merry, crocheting a coaster for the church bazaar in dressing gown, head-scarf and lipstick. She's relaxed and responding well to some half-completed treatment, unconcerned about her hair loss.

There's a highly successful advertising executive, once handsome and athletic, now eaten away and ravaged. His poor scrawny hands grip the arms of a wheelchair pushed by his adoring wife with the now familiar expression of a too-bright smile and devastated eyes. He's goir.g to die.

'Lynne?' I looked up at the nurse, surprised by my name on a stranger's lips. 'Professor Levy will see you now.' And she directed us to an examination cubicle adjacent to the great man's room.

We waited behind a closed door which opened at the hand of a rugged dark-haired, dark-bearded man in an open white coat who said: 'Hi, I'm Ron Levy.'

We shook hands and were joined by a sparkling red-head: 'Dr Sherry Brown, hello. I've heard a lot about you, Lynne.'

'I can explain everything,' and with a soft laugh she shook hands, then: 'Kenneth! We meet at last.' And she took his hand in both of hers and squeezed. They had forged an acquaintance over transatlantic phone calls in the dead of British nights – enquiring, explaining and arranging my present appointment.

A smiling, benign Levy said, 'Before we begin, I'd like the opinion of our Chinese genius,' and sticking his head out of the door he shouted, 'Kwak! Kwak!' (Like the **mating call of a Scottish duck**.) An unusually tall, graceful, oriental man materialised at his side.

After taking my blood pressure and temperature, they took turns to poke, prod and press, then stood gazing down at me with puzzled wonder. I felt like a leg o' lamb at a butcher's banquet.

Was I *sure* I wasn't experiencing any symptoms? No pain? 'No.' No weakness? 'No.' No skin irritation? 'No.' They closed into a scrum and after much teeth-sucking and muttering announced that they'd like to have a new biopsy performed on the splendid, raised node on my thigh. They recommended the Surgicentre and said a Thursday operation would ensure results by next Tuesday. There followed an animated discussion with Kenneth, who eagerly asked pertinent questions and received enthusiastic answers way above my head, leaving me to dress and daydream.

Before we left, they suggested I returned the next day to undergo a 'lymphangiogram' and explained the procedure. It sounded such fun, I could hardly wait.

Friday 20 January

In fact the lymphangiogram turned out to be less arduous than it sounded. I arrived at 9.30 for the 10 o'clock appointment. A delicate oriental nurse washed my feet with antiseptic and chatted while the locally injected anaesthetic took effect. Feet numb, she made a tiny incision – just above my toes – on each foot, found the cotton-thin lymph channels which network the body and inserted two tiny needles. These were tubed to two bottles of pale green dye which, under weighted pressure, travelled up the lymph channels as far as my lower abdomen, filling the infected nodes, thus making any change in size or behaviour easy to spot on X-ray.

The whole three-hour operation was painless but tedious, and I dozed off when the thin white line had progressed as far as my X-rayed knees on the screen in front of me.

José drove a waiting Kenneth and me back to the hotel, and after a snack and two prescribed tablets, my intended afternoon snooze lasted till morning.

14

Sunday 22 January

I awoke on Friday morning, amazed by the result of the previous day's operation. The scar looked so neat and clean, just a thin red line about an inch long, with two little whiskers of self-dissolving twine poking from each end of the internally stitched wound. I heal quickly, but thought it remarkable that I was able to discard the dressing after so short a time. It was completely painless, whereas the tiny, single-stitch wounds on my feet – the result of the lymphangiogram – stung a little.

After breakfast, José took us on a tour of Stanford University and campus. Awesome sandstone buildings, pristine and graced with Moorish arches; as ivy-clad as England, yet unmistakably and respectably American.

A vivid mural of biblical origin covered the gable of a church, partially hidden by red-tile roofs and turrets, and Kenneth decided to investigate further. My leg was beginning to ache a little, so I left him to explore, arranging to meet later at a French restaurant in the shopping precinct.

I had decided to take another look at the Carol Grigg prints. The sole customer, I gazed up at the prints throughout Sade's latest album, while an attractive black proprietor gave me coffee and jived around the empty gallery. On the brink of buying, I reminded myself of my dwindling finances and left, empty-handed, to join Kenneth for an excellent lunch.

The wound on my leg, though not particularly uncomfortable, had begun to swell, so we read and enjoyed a room-service dinner before retiring.

We decided to spend the weekend at the coast, so booked an overnight stay at Half Moon Bay Lodge, sister hotel to the Stanford Park.

Sandy, the lady driver, picked us up after Saturday lunch and during the two-hour trip told us of her struggle to raise a daughter single-handed while trying to build up her 'chauffeur car' business and how after seven years, she'd amassed a fleet of limos, a team of drivers and a drug-addict daughter.

Half Moon Bay is a tiny holiday resort sitting prettily on the coast of northern California. Sandy dropped us outside the basket-chaired reception of a picturesque Spanish ranch hotel, promising to pick us up after lunch on Sunday, and recommended the sweet little Swiss Chalet restaurant next door.

After a relaxing weekend, we were picked up by Sandy at the appointed hour today and as we all had time on our hands, she took us on a tour of the area, starting with a nearby village.

White picket fences surround pastel-painted wooden houses, salt-frosted on the seaward side. A wooden 'doll's house' church with buttermilk walls and a slate-topped spire, a dove-grey schoolhouse with glossy white window-frames and a neat bell tower. We drove round the clean wind-brushed streets, then along miles of coast road edged with indigenous evergreens, strobing a sparkling sea.

We turned on to an unmade road which terminated at a grassy cliff-top, where we parked and strolled along a path to look down at the beach. Jagged grey-white rocks jutted from wet virgin sand and a solitary seabird eyed a boisterous ocean from his driftwood perch.

It looked ancient and unchartered, and Sandy said it was her 'thinking' place. I have a 'thinking' place in Sheffield and I felt distinctly homesick on the drive back to Stanford Park Hotel. **(It's sulphur withdrawal, you need a snort of Tinsley viaduct.)**

A barren moorland road hairpins round a solitary Fox House pub to the Toads Mouth rock, which guards the entrance to the Peak District National Park. Follow the stream through a brackened landscape till the road squeezes between high rock walls of a deep shadowed gully, which spits you into brilliant light at the pinnacle of the highest hill, and there it is, 'The Surprise'; a vast and beautiful valley rolling into the distance, with tiny white houses nestling in the forested foothills and a quilt of fields dipping down to a lazy river.

Strictly speaking, it's in Derbyshire, but Sheffield is blessed with a skirt of spectacular countryside within a few minutes' drive in any direction. Conveniently in the middle of England, you can be in London or Newcastle in the time it takes to get past Chiswick roundabout in the rush hour.

As a kid, I'd stand in a garden of soot-speckled roses listening to the p-poom, p-poom of sheet-metal hammers, echoing across the valley at a distance of four miles. Vibrations tingling the soles of my feet, I'd wait with heart racing for the first sight of an approaching giant, expecting his head to appear above the roof-tops at any second.

When I returned from Scotland as an 8-year-old, the warm smell of the coke ovens was the sweetest scent of all. It vanished along with the soot when the Clean Air Bill came in and Sheffield became the cleanest industrial city in Europe.

Sheffield is peopled with a colourful mixture of characters, not easily impressed and blunt to the point of rudeness at times, but this camouflage is designed to hide a soft heart and a caring nature which is easily taken advantage of. Though they don't suffer fools gladly, in times of trouble they will close round you and nudge you to a safe place, keeping marauders at bay until you recover.

My extensive travels have revealed no place I would rather be. It's home.

On our return, crowds of cheering hotel visitors and staff spilled out of every lounge and bar, where gigantic T.V.s spewed live coverage of the Superbowl Football Contest, and the San Francisco Forty-Niners (**local lads**) looked like pulling it off.

Over Kenneth's shoulder and a tray of burgers and Budweiser, I watched a screen full of hulking, helmeted Frankensteins, lumbering after some poor fool who's trying to make off with their ball. Upon catching him, they hurl him to the ground and the entire team falls on him, forming a squirming man-pile of thrusting buttocks and flailing fists. They then beat him soundly until he apologises.

Wednesday 25 January

Continuous news coverage of the huge jubilant throngs
crowding the streets dashed our hopes of visiting San
Francisco on Monday. They were gathered to witness the
victory parade. Just as well, really; my biopsy wound was
hard and raised to the size of a ping-pong ball. So I took
Kenneth's advice and spent the day in bed. My morning
was brightened when an early birthday card was pushed
under the door along with the newspapers. It was from
Lynda; I'm knocked out that she thought of sending it to
America.

Lynda's concern has been touching and genuine and
her support equal to Pam's and Malc's. A decent, good
woman, without an ounce of cunning or guile, she hasn't
been forgiven by some for committing the sin of falling
helplessly in love. She's easy to talk to and still as lovely
as the first time we met her.

*It was her mouth I noticed first, full and voluptuous, pouting
beneath a cute little nose and enormous brown eyes. Dark tendrils of hair escaped from a pink headscarf and curled round her
face, sticking in places to golden heat-moistened skin. She was
like a beautiful gypsy in the headscarf and full cotton skirt,
white top and hoop earrings.*

*She swayed towards us with a languid grace, a warm smile
and an outstretched hand, her lovely figure moving in all the
right places and the sun glinting off a fine gold ankle-chain. (Oh
dear! A dark-haired, dark-eyed endomorph.)*

*I could hear Malc's heart flipping around in his rib-cage
and wasn't at all surprised by a Paul Robeson voice saying, 'Hi!
I'm Malcolm.'*

'Lynda,' she smiled, then, 'You must be Lynne. Patrick's

messing around with the barbecue. Come on through.' With difficulty she extracted her hand from Malc's, who'd forgotten to let
go, and we followed her past a beam-exposed stone cottage to the
soft springy grass of an orchard, polka-dot gay with red apples.

Georgina – a Great Dane – and Will-Will – a black Labra-
dor – guarded the two-year-old twins, Daniel and Lucie, and
Patrick Crapper, her estate agent husband. We'd met Patrick
shortly after my 'New Faces' victory, when he helped us find our
new home 'Tanglewood', a quirky old bungalow set in 25 acres of
National Park land.

The house needed drastic modernisation and Patrick had invited us to Sunday lunch to inspect the work of Ron Walker, the
architect, who'd sensitively converted their cottage. Patrick is an
irresistibly attractive man, dapper and wiry with an I.Q. in the
highest 2 per cent, a keen sense of the ridiculous and repartee delivered with the speed of an auctioneer. A born clown, mimic and
raconteur, he's probably the most amusing man I've ever met and
must be hell to live with.

I was recovering from a recent nose job (after seeing it for
the first time on T.V., I immediately had a foot and a half
snipped off the end). With black eyes, a Beatle wig and a swollen face, I had no chance of outdazzling the lovely Lynda, but I
gained Malc's attention occasionally and fleetingly with the odd
caustic comment:

'Is that steak too rare for you, Lynne?'

'Rare! It's just eaten my cabbage.'

Malc was never a sports fanatic. The only field games he indulged in were the ones at the back of the fire station and he
thought racquets were the result of calcium deprivation. Understandably, gales of laughter greeted him when, three days aft..r
their first meeting, he came prancing into the kitchen in tennis
whites and plimsolls with a racquet under his arm, having
arranged a game of squash with Lynda.

It heralded the beginning of love and cartilage trouble, and he's still afflicted by both. He was willing to give up the hard-earned success he rightfully shared with me, to pursue his own hopes and ambitions. I was so busy riding the crest of my long-awaited wave, it never occurred to me he might want a wave of his own. Lynda likewise was willing to relinquish an easy life of nannies, Club Med holidays and respectability to share a small flat above a butcher's shop with the man she loved and her twins. They deserved happiness. Why should I stand in their way?

Perhaps it was time to spread my wings, see how far I could fly without the weight of responsibility. I did nothing to discourage the affair and a painless and amicable divorce allowed our friendship to continue and grow.

In May of 1978, Lynda moved into 'Tanglewood' with the twins and I moved out to start a 22-week summer season on the North Pier at Blackpool. John took over the bookkeeping and bill-paying from Malc and made life as easy as possible for me. I gave him power of attorney and relied on him to govern my expenditure. When it got too high, he would confiscate my credit cards.

I would return to 'Tanglewood' each Sunday to visit the kids. Strangely enough, it felt perfectly natural and there was never any animosity, which made it easier on the kids and all concerned.

When my summer season ended I moved in with John and his wife Marcia until I found the flat.

I missed Malc almost mortally for years. He and Lynda were happy. I was convinced I had allowed the only Real man on earth to slip through my fingers. It was only when I met Kenneth in the last week of 1984 that I realised the truth of 'everything happens for the best'.

It was Professor Levy who delivered the dramatic news at

the Tuesday cancer clinic.

He said the results of the biopsy had confirmed Dr Kwak's opinion of my original biopsy slides. I had only a small percentage of the non-aggressive but incurable follicular lymphoma, the majority of the disease was an aggressive, fast-spreading type that stood a 50 per cent chance of complete cure with aggressive chemotherapy, which hopefully would wipe out the incurable type as well.

He said there was a thin line between non-aggressive, intermediate and aggressive lymphoma, but the treatment and prognosis varied greatly. My rare, but not unique, lack of symptoms had clouded the issue initially, but now he was convinced I should return home immediately and commence chemotherapy.

'We were thinking of going to Florida for a few . . .'

'IMMEDIATELY!'

'And if I don't have chemotherapy?'

'You'll be dead in eighteen months.'

We returned to the hotel and booked the first available flight back to Heathrow.

Kenneth was high on hope. For the first time since diagnosis I'd been offered a chance of life and, full of *joie de vivre*, he whisked me across the road to a fascinating shop called 'The Three Sisters'.

It contained books on the occult, jewellery with curative properties, icons and crystals and earthenware fertility goddesses, tarot cards and fool's gold, rune stones and Indian fortune sticks. There were couches and cups beside a bubbling coffee-pot and we browsed happily, leaving with a bag full of 'Positive Thinking' tapes and 'Cure Yourself of Cancer' books, along with assorted mumbo-jumbo, an hour and a half later.

On Wednesday morning, I mentioned the Carol Grigg prints to Kenneth who said he was sure we could get them home okay, if I really wanted them, so after packing, I limped across to the precinct and bought the prints, leaving them in the gallery while I purchased yards of bubble-wrap, brown paper and plastic tape. Getting them back to the hotel was horse work; they were heavy and cumbersome and the string carrying-handle bit into my fingers, but leading with my Scottish chin, I struck out with determination and finally reached my destination with purple fingers and a throbbing leg.

Kenneth was furious. (**You neglected to mention they were ready framed.**) He had expected me to arrive with a cardboard tube full of curled-up prints. He called me a stupid, stubborn woman, and stormed off to the bar.

15

Thursday 26 January
My birthday – home again

It's fantastic to be back home. And no one knows except the family. Great. No press. I didn't sleep last night on the 'plane, but finished my Jackie Collins and watched half a Bruce Willis film (another night of achievement).

I had a yen to make a spaghetti bolognese when we finally black-cabbed to the cottage, and asked poor Kenneth to go down to the village and collect the necessary. I had a glorious time. It reminded me of when Jeff Ritcher, my choreographer, came to dinner:

It was at the height of my dancing career (your what?!!). I was out to impress. (God always boots you up the bum when you're posing.) The bolognese was ready – bits of red pepper and carrot to give it that Carrier-esque quality (and help disguise the grease.) Table ready, dressed to kill, Mary Chess and Mozart filling the air, doorbell rings, missing false nail – it's in the bolognese, I know for sure.

I broddle about in the bolognese without luck, then let Jeff in. I ply him with wine and watch every mouthful he takes. (Was that a carrot or a nail? Oh, my God!) The next day I felt honour-bound to tell him that if anyone goosed him from the inside – it was me.

False nails – another era.

I opened a few birthday cards, played music, enjoyed the view, read a little and felt as high as a kite all day. Rang Graham Roberts, an old and dear friend, for a few minutes that lasted hours. Really enjoyed it, we talked philosophy. (**This is the lady who thought Bertrand Russell ran a circus?**)

The lump has taken on spectacular proportions and the feet are a bit puffy as well. Kenneth wants to play doctors and examine said lump. I'm a shade reluctant – I've seen him fix a plug. 'Yuck! Yuck!' and cries of 'Claim a refund!' fill the examining room that was once our kitchen. I caught his alarm for a split second, before he very sensibly suggested we rang the Surgicentre and spoke to Dr Eisenstat.

He reassured us both completely: it was lymph fluid. In removing the largest node, he'd nicked a smaller one and the lymph fluid had gathered under the weakest point, the scar, hence the hardness and the odd shape. Phew!!

I'm too high to sleep. I potter about and listen to a 'Positive Thinking' tape we bought in that weird little shop in Stanford. It makes a lot of sense. I still feel so happy, I can touch my soul. I'm so aware. Oh! And I'm forty-four! (**Forty-four and one day.**) A rosy glow has just lit the Constable outside. Life is terrific. I hope I always feel as alive as this.

When we saw Dr McKenzie on Friday he was well acquainted with the American findings, after lengthy phone calls with Professor Levy, and was delighted with the results. It's gratifying to know how eagerly they are prepared to work with each other, given the opportunity.

He examined the swollen scar and confirmed that it was just lymph fluid, which could be aspirated or left to its own devices. As it wasn't troubling me, he decided on the latter.

The second question of the day was chemotherapy. There are several different combinations of drugs, usually administered fortnightly over a six-month period, and occasionally weekly over a three-month period. He said he rather favoured the longer treatment as it gave the white cells more time to recover.

He wanted to begin treatment on Monday, but I begged him for an extra week, I'm so homesick for Sheffield (it's no use trying to escape) and feel a visit would burnish my fighting mettle. It was agreed that treatment would begin on Monday week.

I prefer motorways after midnight, so, after washing and ironing and freezing some home-made soup for Kenneth (salmonella on a stick) I set off for Sheffield at 11.45 p.m. on Saturday and arrived in the town centre at 2.30 on Sunday morning to find it buzzing with nightlife.

I'd forgotten that Sheffield had moved into the eighties, and waited in small traffic queues while throngs of late-night revellers used pelican crossings. A clutch of bow-ties, tiaras and musquash waited for chauffeurs outside the Cutlers' Hall. A bunch of charm bracelets, taffeta frills and Debenham wigs gathered outside the Grosve-

'For a short time, life was bliss. I was a proper mom at last, there when the kids came home from school with time to listen to them.'

Opposite: '... "So, with 98 points, Marti Caine is the outright winner of *New Faces 1975*" and Cinderella went to the ball.'

'"M" is more than a mere dressmaker, she's an artist, a fairy godmother sewing with enchanted thread... some have caused quite a furore in the past.' (photo: Ben Jones)

Above: 'I'm playing the evil Red Queen in a play about Snow White this year. It's a wonderful part – sort of Margaret Thatcher without the vulnerability.'

Left: 'Mass adoration is a highly addictive drug. I was hooked. I knew my singing was not good enough to evoke that kind of response from an audience. The only way to do it was as a comic.'

Opposite: '… I selected my favourite gown – black silk "Spanish" job with roses under the flared cap sleeves. (Nina once said "you looked as though you had a couple of allotments under your arms").'

'I can hear Kenneth running his bath, we leave for the airport at six. His briefcase bulges on the table, full of slides and biopsy reports... if it hadn't been for his diligent research... I wouldn't be leaving for America and the hope of a cure. I think God sent Kenneth.'

Opposite: '... after *New faces* my career continued to thrive, far longer than my original esitmate of three years.' (photo: Brian Aries)

'"What is the average life-expectancy of someone with follicular lymphoma?" "Five years, but I would expect you to do better." How does live for ever grab you, Doc?' (photo: Trevor Leighton)

nor and trilled 'Cooee' to a set of mohair suits and medallioned chests. A Porsche full of San Tropez suntans throbbed outside Josephine's night club and hair-gelled, pierce-eared, nail-biters in the uniform of youth walked in arm-linked lines, happy and harmless. How the old place has changed.

It was almost 3 a.m., when I let myself into the flat: I love it. It's always so clean and warm. I feel safe.

The decor is a mixture of 'high tech' – stainless steel ceilings, slate surfaces and Titzio lamps; Japanese – sunken bed, no clutter and ikebana flower arrangements; and Art Nouveau – a Mackintosh chair, a Corbusier chaise-longue and a black and pink colour scheme.

I made coffee, pottered around and waited for dawn, watching the panoramic spread of twinkling city lights, like a mini-Manhattan, from a south-facing glass wall in my lounge.

It's like returning to the womb.

I'd finished my summer season in Blackpool and had been living with John and his family for about four months, house-hunting when time permitted, but so far hadn't found a place that felt right.

It was John who mentioned a flat for sale in a prestigious block within walking distance of his home. I didn't want to be a flat dweller, I wanted solitude and a garden. Living in the isolated splendour of 'Tanglewood', I'd grown accustomed to the delights of playing music as loud as I wanted and hoovering at four in the morning if the need arose, and I didn't fancy buying myself a load of rules and restrictions.

To please John, I strolled the short distance to the flat with him. We took the lift to the third floor, rang the bell and were ushered into a wide hallway. It was instant love. I didn't need to see any more – the decor wasn't my style anyway – it was the feel of the place.

I moved in with nothing but big ideas. Malc and I had come to an amicable agreement about our collective possessions (he kept 'em!). He kept everything until I got a place of my own, when I collected the things I wanted. By this time Malc had sold 'Tanglewood' and bought a butcher's shop with a flat above and was doing well. He was happy and able, at last, to fulfil his own ambitions.

Lee had joined the Royal Marine Commandos and Max had taken his place in the butcher's shop with Malc. Roger moved into my flat along with an army of workmen who, under the direction of Ron Walker – the architect Patrick Crapper had introduced us to – proceeded to raise floors, lower ceilings and sink baths.

The flat became my reason for living and I threw myself into work to pay for my new obsession, afraid to finish it in case I was left with nothing to live for. I was becoming more and more insular. I found I was inhibited by men and unsure whether it was me or Marti Caine they wanted, so I stayed home and played house in my semi-luxurious padded cell, safe from the feeling of panic that waited outside.

Africa happened at just the right time. I was uninformed, knew nothing about 'puppet states', but had heard the odd thing about the anti-apartheid movement on the radio, so I checked with Equity who said it was O.K. to go, as Sun City was in Bophuthatswana, a 'homeland' ruled by President Mangopi.

Sun City was 'Fantasy Island'. A man-made garden of Eden with blue lagoons and perfect palm trees, abundant with every indulgence known to man – except sex. It was on show, in the shape of glamorous showgirls and gorgeous dancers, but NEVER for sale. Sun City was family entertainment, a posh Butlins with safe fun for kids, grans, mums and dads as well as serious gamblers. The nickname 'Sin City' was an invention of the narrow-minded Afrikaner with his Dutch Reform Church morality who deemed gambling and the show of a white nipple sinful, but nonetheless crossed the border in droves.

Sun City was against all South African principles. Black, white, brown and yellow worked, lived and played together. They married and raised families and neighboured each other in neat bungalows. President Mangopi, though I'm sure he had his enemies, was popular. He built roads, schools and hospitals; the local Swana were wealthier and held responsible positions and a truly multiracial harmony existed, a fine example of how things COULD be.

Necessary trips to Johannesburg forced the real situation upon us. Our black American and African colleagues were pushed off pavements, ordered out of restaurants and refused admittance to cinemas. The white contingent suffered bitter shame and guilt and our outraged outbursts did nothing to make things better.

Had I been fully informed of the situation, I would never have gone to Africa. By going I experienced the horror of apartheid for myself vicariously through close black friends. I got to know the Swana people and learned a little of their language. The sight of a 7,000-strong black audience holding candles aloft with solemn dignity for George Benson's 'The Greatest Love' will stay with me for ever. I was privy to a culture where the old were revered and cared for by all the tribe, where the wisest matriarch manipulated the string of an apparently patriarchal society and where the witch doctor sang gospel songs before conducting some pagan rite learned thousands of years before Christianity eroded his culture.

On one such occasion, the Sun City security police had questioned all eighty-odd of the dancers, showgirls and spec-acts that made up the cast of the multi-million-pound extravaganza we were appearing in. Two hundred and fifty Rand, the proceeds of a wedding gift whip-round, had been stolen from a dressing room and we were all under suspicion, including the hundred or so black dressers and stage-hands. So far investigations had revealed nothing, suspicion falling on the dressers on the grounds of opportunity.

Mr Wagner, a gifted Austrian hotelier and manager of the complex, had worked with the Swanas for fifteen years. He liked and respected them and understood their tribal customs. Detecting the prickly unrest among the dressers, he stepped forward and said, 'This is not a police matter. We must send for the witch doctor.'

The Swanas regarded Wagner as a King Solomon, and this decision was applauded by the much relieved dressers. The innocent shall sleep, the guilty toss wretchedly – and with that thought, we all returned home. A meeting was arranged for the next day at the scene of the crime between Simon – the witch doctor – and Mr Wagner, head dancer, head showgirl, ballet master, head dresser and myself.

Wagner and I arrived earlier than most and over coffee in the privacy of my dressing room, I asked if he'd formed any opinions.

'The witch doctor will sort it out,' he said with a straight face.

'You're joking.' I giggled, fascinated nonetheless.

'Wait and see,' he said.

I didn't have to wait long before Simon arrived resplendent as a showgirl, in feathered skirt and head-dress, arm and leg bracelets, bone necklace and tribal trim. He carried an odd-shaped staff in one hand and an ancient, ornate rattle in the other.

Back-stage of the extravaganza theatre was vast, with a warren of corridors and stairs leading to hangar-sized wardrobe rooms, hair-dressing salons, physiotherapy rooms, showers and rows of ten-seater dressing rooms as well as single suites like my own. Simon wanted to begin in the wardrobes for some reason, so we followed the select party through the labyrinth.

Thick 20-foot poles jutted into the vast wardrobe rooms, custom built to hang the head-dresses worn in the show – some as much as 18 feet across. Harnessed creations of feather, diamanté and crystal perched in neat rows like colourful prehistoric vultures pecking at rows of grass skirts. There were rows of ostrich fans, space helmets, swords and shields, bangles and beads, matador capes and a spectacular row of iridescent butterfly wings with a twenty-foot span. All manner of glitzy showbiz paraphernalia spilled from the walls of the wardrobe rooms, and a frenzied riot of colour and texture seemed to thrust itself at us as we entered.

The costumes were hanging in order of appearance and only a dresser knew which girl wore which costume in which routine and in what order. Silence fell as Simon began to make tuneless humming sounds and, clearing the way with his staff, danced into the rows of finery, touching each garment with his rattle and shaking it now and then. He emerged trance-like and breathless and took a few moments to regain his composure before voicing his findings to the assembled gathering.

'The thief is the wearer of this skirt,' he declared dramatically, with the accent on this, and the skirt was handed to him by a dresser.

'This hat.' He indicated with his staff and the hat was proffered, and so on until he had a small collection of articles which he threw to the ground and carefully stepped on, beckoning Mr Wagner who bent to examine the name-tags sewn into each item.

They all bore the same name.

The hairs stood up on the back of my neck and, as if further proof was needed, Simon proceeded to whizz through the dress-

ing rooms shouting, 'The thief sits on this chair. The thief uses
this towel, this brush, this mirror . . .'

Again, they belonged to the same person. I was incredulous,
but Mr Wagner said he'd seen this and stranger things happen
and, as far as he was concerned, the matter was closed. We
couldn't accuse the culprit on such unscientific evidence, of
course, but the assembled cast were told of the events of the day,
omitting only the name of the thief who left within a week com-
plaining of home-sickness.

The sun crept up and lit the low cloud that seems to
gather beneath my hill-top balcony every morning,
blocking out the surrounding roof-tops and blanketing
the garden in mist so that only the poplar tops poke
through. It's like drifting in space on a private planet and
a languid tranquillity lulls me to sleep.

Tuesday 31 January

Monday – I cleaned an already clean flat and James
Mackintosh, my next-door neighbour, cooked dinner for
me. James must be one of the most eligible bachelors in
Sheffield – six-two, film-star looks, successful and single
with a passion for fast cars and women.

Romantically, we got off on the wrong foot from
square one. It was the day I moved into the flat.

I was unpacking the mementoes of eighteen years of marriage (a
box of chalk Alsatians – Mother's Day gifts – and a box of toi-
letries). It was during my puce hair phase and I sat on the hall
floor emptying the contents of the toiletry box with bright purple
'Crazy Colour' hair dye running down my face and neck, adding

new colour to my multi-streaked hair-dying dressing-gown.

I came across an ancient tube of Veet hair remover and, just for the hell of it, smeared an odious dollop on my top lip. The smell made my eyes run and black mascara tracks contrasted nicely with the rivulets of hair dye against the white, stinking moustache.

A battery-operated toothbrush, short of batteries, rested on my knee while I struggled to remove new batteries from a vibrator as big as a thermos flask that Malc had packed as a joke.

I couldn't figure out how to undo the battery compartment, and only succeeded in turning it on. It was at this stage that James walked in. Consequently, our relationship has never been anything but platonic.

Today was Max's day off, so we drove into Derbyshire for lunch, dined on Marks and Spencer at the flat and watched a couple of videos.

Pam and I have arranged a girls' day out tomorrow and as I don't have an alarm clock with me, she's promised to give me a wake-up call in the morning.

Wednesday 1 February (4 a.m. – so it's Thursday)
Sheffield flat

I've had a great day. Weather springy, air fizzy. Battled with the phone and the make-up mirror all morning after Pam's disgustingly chirpy – geared to grate – alarm call at 10.30. I was at the stage where I'm trying to stop the lip-line running up the nose when the door-bell rang – it was Sandy, another neighbour. Six foot, suntanned and gorgeous, she followed me down the hall bathing me in Yorkshire accent and plonked down in the chair opposite. Looking like the front of *Harper's and Queen,* she said, 'If tha't doin' nowt cumore an' we'll get bleedin' pissed!' **(I really like that woman!)**

I'm late for Pam. I'm looking good. **(You've got ten bob on yourself, haven't you?)** Grey Escada and grey cashmere polo, black sombrero, black hoop earrings, snakeskin spikes and a fist full of wonderful tan and black tiger-stripe chiffon scarf. Giving it full monti and a touch of Lady Di, I climbed elegantly out of my car and wiggled across the forecourt for the benefit of a plumber and his young mate, who were tampering with Pam's pipes. **(You're such a tacky tart!)**

I know it seems a shade salacious, but masculinity deserves femininity – if it's got a monkey wrench in its hand, it's masculine – so I wiggle a little. So what? Admittedly, it's overkill for the young guy – his jaw drops simultaneously with his spanner, and his eyes bulge simultaneously with his Levi's. The older man doesn't bat an eyelid, and says, 'She'll not be needing you today, love, window cleaner's just been!' Cheek!

She's been ready for an hour, I can tell, and she looks terrific in the blue suit and spikes. No rush, we laze about with Eric, drinking coffee and revelling in the ease of each other, not talking particularly, before waving goodbye to Eric and heading for Eckington and a shoe-shop that advertises in *Vogue!*

Thanks to Pam's navigating and my driving, the ten-minute drive only took us an hour and a half, so we did quite well really. We had similar success finding the car park and after our fourth circuit of the town, small groups were gathering to wave.

In desperation we drove up an alley leading to a garage yard housing all the scrap from World War Two and four assorted mechanics. Pam got out and tottered across the yard oozing femininity and began, '"Scuse me lads. . . .' By the time I reversed round she'd ascertained the whereabouts of the car park and the shoe-shop that advertises in *Vogue,* and had arranged for cups of Earl Grey in china cups to be brought while we waited for a free service. (**She wastes no time, that girl!**)

As he pumped air into the front tyre one of the mechanics observed: 'That front wheel's falling off!' and instructed the one cleaning the windscreen to come and offer a second opinion.

'That front wheel's falling off!' observed the second man. Fred was called and finally Albert. The four vanished from view beyond the rim of our tea-cups as they squatted down to tug on the wheel.

Albert bobbed into view. 'That front wheel's falling off!' Convinced of a wind-up, we climbed out of our leathered luxury and squatted down to squash this foul rumour . . . the front wheel *was* falling off!

'Do you think it will get us to the shoe-shop?' enquired Pam.

'The one that advertises in *Vogue*?'

We nodded.

'It might.'

'That's O.K. then!' we said in unison, thanked them for the tea, the advice and the free service and squeaked off!

We parked the car on double yellows and set off across the cobbled pedestrian precinct to find the Eckington shoe-shop that advertises in *Vogue*. A lewd, loud wolf-whistle rent the air.

'That's mine.'

'No, it's not – he was looking at me.'

We stopped a woman.

'Could you tell us where the shoe-shop is?'

'The one that advertises in *Vogue*?'

'Yes!'

'It's closed!'

That 'spend or kill' look crept into Pam's eyes and I knew I had to get her to a boutique as quickly as possible. To cheer her up, I put a ten pence piece into a slot beneath a colourful caged parrot outside a shop – a lewd, loud wolf whistle rent the air. Soon we were falling over each other in our haste to exercise the plastic.

I bought a strapless navy Escada dress. I look horrendous in it! I'm going to pin it on the bedroom wall and determine to look stunning in it this time next year, on holiday, in Barbados. Pam didn't buy anything, she said, but nonetheless left the shop with legs buckling under the weight of several large carrier-bags full of gear.

We all went to dinner – Pam, Eric, Linda, Malc and me – to 'Mr C's' in Chesterfield. Malc complained about his backache and his cartilage problem, and it was decided that this was God's exquisite justice. His wedding tackle would remain in gloriously tumescent working order until he was 90, but his back and knees had gone at 40.

It's 5.30 a.m. – again. **(This is no way to look after yourself.)** I don't want to waste time sleeping.

16

Thursday 2 February

An infuriating telephone jangled me into wakefulness at 10 a.m. It was Kenneth. Dr McKenzie wanted to see me at the Hammersmith Hospital at 4 p.m. today. My heart sank. I intended to stay a little longer. (You're just trying to evade the inevitable, wimp.)

After a leisurely breakfast and shower, I dressed, packed and hit the road. A David Sandbourn and Marcus Miller 'live' album made my drive pleasant and I finally arrived at the Hammersmith Hospital to a now avuncular Dr McKenzie at 3.45 p.m.

He shocks me by announcing he's decided to go for the *three*-month treatment. He explains the reason for his change of mind is due to the fact that I have two types of lymphoma at the same time, which puts me in a 3 per cent bracket (thank God it's nothing common) and the faster therapy should eradicate the non-aggressive but supposedly incurable type as well as the aggressive, fast-spreading variety. He is going to use an aggressive chemo-cocktail called PACE-BOM, administered alternately – PACE on week one, BOM on week two and so on, for twelve weeks. The name is derived from the initials of the drugs used: prednisolone (an orally administered steroid), adriamycin, cyclophosphamide and etoposide (V.Pl6), alternated with bleomycin, oncovin (vincristine) and methotrexate. **(So now you know.)** He seems reluctant to answer my questions on side effects, saying everyone reacts differently but relaxation and attitude were the keys to an easy time.

Friday 3 February
(Queen's Gardens)

I've made an appointment to see David Taylor, my accountant. The wolves are baying. Thank God most of my tax is paid, but the fact remains that there's an overdraft, weighty mortgages to pay, and no work in the book for either of us. Money has never bothered me, I've concluded that too much of it is worse than too little **(that's 'cos you're an expert at being skint)** and I make a point of spending what's left after expenses as quickly as possible.

I work when I want, eat when I want, sleep when I want **(a blessing indeed!)**. Life is rosy, but never cushy enough to become complacent. Anyway, money falls from the sky. **(She says, complacently.)**

It was Christmas Eve. We were living in the prefab in Scotland. My Mam was out of her pills and was doing cold turkey curled up in a corner clutching a hot-water-bottle, rocking to and fro and retching. We were cold and hungry and completely skint. In the fatter days of a few months earlier, a 'friend' used to visit her, a Polish surgeon – Dr K – he called every Friday bearing gifts of bath oil, perfume or a silk scarf, tins of Polish sausage and cabbage, schnapps and always a box of Terry's 'All Gold' chocolates. We hated dark chocolate – and these being the days of plenty, piled the boxes in a rarely used cupboard and forgot about them – till now. 'The chocolates!' I leap up, climb on a chair and remove the first box from a pile on the top shelf. I take the lid off – no cellophane, just a lift-off lid and there, sandwiched between the corrugated paper and the soft 'Contents' pad is a large white, perfectly smooth £5 note. Every box – about a dozen – contained one. All the shops were shut, but what a New Year!

I have no desire to store up millions (**you speak for yourself**). I trust in fate.

Speaking of fate, a strange thing has happened. Jill Ireland's book has just arrived from her publisher, with a letter asking if I would be interested in writing a similar thing. I might! I could start making notes from this diary. Funny, I was only thinking about it yesterday. I phone and make an appointment for 4 o'clock – that gives me half an hour – then off to see David Taylor. I really must do something about this pencilled scrawl. Get a typist or something. He's not going to be very impressed by this Woolies notepad.

I called at Peter Jones in Sloane Street to replace two beautiful Cusinoux saucepans I'd burnt. I shall know better than to cook in them in future! I also bought Kenneth a new egg pan; he's good at egg soldiers and I felt his equipment needed upgrading. I clanked round Sloane Square and sat in Oriels watching the beautiful people over strong coffee and Michael Franks – nice!

I caught a cab to the publishers in Covent Garden. Time to push open the doors of opportunity. They were double doors, glass ones, belonging to a modern five-storey block – all theirs! Gulp! I expected a couple of rooms above a greasy café. I waved a tenner at the cab driver and persuaded him to wait for me – I can't go clanking in there with a set of saucepans under my arm.

Joan Collins, almost as glossy as life, pouted at me from behind the tall letters of *Prime Time* and I accidentally stumbled upon reception. A secretary escorted me to a high-speed lift which decanted me on to the fourth floor while my stomach was still on the second.

I read the publisher a few pages of my diary. I could only study him peripherally, as I was intent on hiding the embarrassment of my audition, but my antennae picked up a sudden gear-change.

Was it my imagination, or did he like what he was hearing? He seemed to – he talked of an advance (**thank you, fairy godmother**) and 6,000 words and serial rights and contracts, and exited to have the few pages I'd read out photocopied.

5 o'clock. Time for David Taylor, the magic otter. I love David. He's alive and aware and a wizard of tax consultancy. He's soft-spoken, unassuming and always reasonable. He enjoys his work, he's a Sherlock Holmes, a Poirot, a super sleuth tracking down the legal loophole. He offers alternatives and possibilities, views long- and short-term, and puts things into perspective.

A mystical light seemed to glow from his ledgers and illuminate his pleasant face, as he informed me that things were pretty desperate and I would need more than the promise of an advance to refill the coffers. On the brighter side, my insurance policies and my will are sorted out at last and if I die before 1992, the boys will be O.K. (**Bully for them.**) Just enough to ensure their future without robbing them of a sense of achievement.

2 *a.m.* What an exciting day. Today I started a new career. I am now a professional writer, or will be when the advance comes through (**don't count your chickens**). It's just what I need to help me through chemo – earning on my back (**Mummy will be pleased!**).

The only problem now is how to keep the bank manager happy until the royalties start rolling in.

Monday 6 February

Just got time to stuff some gear into a bag. The glossy yellow of a General Trading Company bag catches my eye, and I empty the contents of the Louis Vuitton holdall into it. One pair of M. & S. thermal 'jamas. One size-22 candlewick dressing-gown (**that's your York-shire/Scots streak – huge dressing-gowns are better value for money**) and ever-ready soap-bag. Black spikes and trousers. Large tweed jacket with pink blouse. We're off – see you later, house!

Kenneth's driving – I'm clearing my handbag out. The car is a tip. I'm ashamed of myself. (**How come someone with immaculate cupboards can keep a car like this?**) I clear a space in the debris, tip the accumulated rubbish out of my bag and begin to rummage. Kenneth is whistling. In four years of marriage, I've never heard him whistle before. He's nervous. Four years! The 6th of February. My God! It's our wedding anniversary – we'd both forgotten. **(Perhaps a candle-lit battle for two later?)**

In no time at all we're fighting for a parking space outside the Cromwell, then striding purposefully through its wide-corridored opulence to our duly appointed reception area.

'Ah, Mrs Ives' – the beautiful Philippino nurse with the smile – 'Come with me and I'll take a little blood.' I took a step forward, Kenneth a step back, but eventually both followed the nurse to a small outpatients' ward. Beside the nurses' station was a trolley bearing a cold steel tray of sharp cruel points. Kenneth's foot found a caster and the instruments clattered together, screaming protest and swearing vengeance. **(You're too fanciful for your own good, you.)**

'No need to take your blouse off, Mrs Ives, just roll up your sleeve.' Kenneth started to whistle again.

'Why don't you go now, love, come and see me later; bring me some grapes in an air sickbag.' I think he was grateful to be let off the hook and backed out waving, saying, 'Good luck. Enjoy it!?!'

'Now, one little prick and it's all over.' **(Story of every woman's life.)** And it was. She skilfully inserted a thin tube into my forearm attached to a multi-headed nozzle affair, called a 'cannula', which would accommodate various syringes and drips, with no need to stick anything else into me. That's a relief!

She taped the cannula snugly to my arm and I forgot it was there as I scooped up my jacket and collected my bags. 'I'll be up later to give you your treatment!' The smile remained constant, but her eyelids fluttered.

A chirpy porter led me to the lift and up to the third floor, where a nurse smiled reassuringly and said, 'Mrs

Ives? You're in 310 – follow me, please.' We walked past a modern American nursing station, from which four corridors of discreet double-doored private rooms led off. From the open ones came the awful sound of retching: welcome to the chemo ward! I'm scared (**wimp, wimp, wimp – coward**). It's the fear of the unknown (**but it's Hobson's choice, girl**). It's like having a baby. I cheered myself a little with this thought. Even at 17 I found childbirth an uplifting experience (**you weren't supposed to find it uplifting in Shiregreen in the sixties!**). All I was supposed to feel was pain, guilt and shame. Maybe chemo will be the same. (**Wait and see. Don't expect the worst, and you won't get it.**)

3 o'clock. I'm in my room. It's pleasant, like a small hotel room, en-suite bathroom and loo, omnipresent Sony, locker and a bed that 'did things' at the press of a button.

3.30. Chest X-ray and electro-cardiograph.

4 o'clock. The Philippino nurse walks in with a discreetly covered tray. 'Food?' I ask, knowing it not to be. 'Are you hungry?' she asks with concern. I am, now I think about it, starving! It never occurred to me that one could eat before a treatment. I am assured that it makes no difference, and coffee and a chicken sandwich arrive.

An efficient army bustles in and out taking temperature and blood pressure for the ten minutes it takes to eat the sandwich (**not easy with a strategically placed thermometer**). The parade is brought to a finale by a delightful, slightly camp, male nurse bearing (**no, not an enema**) a 'cold cap'. This is a two-inch-thick bathing cap filled with what feels like heavy frozen jelly. It is supposed to fit tightly over the head while the drugs are being administered. We develop an instant rapport while discussing the dubious merits of said cap. It is supposed to help reduce hair loss, although with the combination of drugs I am using hair loss is inevitable.

I'll tell you something, cancer really straightens out your priorities. I'm a vain woman but to be honest, I don't care if my nose falls off, as long as I live.

I politely decline the cap. Male nurse agrees and bids me a fond farewell. He's off on his hols to Tenerife for a fortnight, but says he'll look forward to my fourth treatment when he'll be brown and back. I don't have the heart to tell him that Tenerife has just had its first snowfall in thirty years.

I am left alone for a few minutes to practise my relaxation routine.

4.30-ish. Let battle commence. The nurse attaches a saline drip to one of the nozzles before administering the first drug via another. The chemical is red – adriamycin – and will take about ten minutes to go in. It may burn the vein a little, if so I am to let her know and she'll flush it through with the saline. O.K.? We chat for ten minutes. I feel nothing. Then a burning sensation. I tell her. She immediately adjusts the saline drip and the burning sensation stops. Five minutes later the second drug, cyclophosphamide, is attached to the nozzle. A slight metallic taste hits my throat briefly and that's all. The third drug – etoposide – is in a small drip-bag suspended along with the saline, followed by an 'anti-puke' drug called maxolon. It's 4.50.

'Is that it?' I ask.

'Yes, that's it.' Except for six pints of saline.

'When do I start to throw up?' She laughs and places a disposable vomit tray on my bedside table. It doesn't look very big – I wonder if she knows about the chicken sandwich?

5.30. I'm alone. Nothing's happening, I feel fine – I ring Kenneth and report. He can't keep the relief out of his voice. I ring Lynda and Pam and report – so far, so good.

Nothing on telly and the 'in house' movie is drawing to a close. I pick up a Ruth Rendell mystery and put it down. Then in bored desperation press one of the buttons on the bed that 'does things'. Over the next five minutes I, my pillows and bottom sheet slid slowly down the incontinence-proof mattress while the bed juddered and whined to a sitting position. A pale arthritic Frankenstein. It is at this high point that my dinner of lentil soup, roast beef and etceteras, cheese, biscuits, coffee and mints arrives. I demolish it, more out of boredom than hunger, grab my disposable vomit tray and wait – nothing – not even a burp.

7 o'clock. I've abandoned my vomit tray and am now exhausted, with my finger on the button of the bed that does things, waiting for it to return to the horizontal position. My drip-pipe is stretched to the limit and my pillow about to slip out of bed, my thermal 'jamas are under my armpits and clinging to various crevices when Dr McKenzie walks in.

After rearranging myself, we talk for half an hour about him and his, me and mine and the drugs that have just been administered.

McKenzie leaves. I feel fine. The room is warm and I feel drowsy. Kenneth bounds in with a carrier-bag full of orange peel and grape stalks. His enthusiasm lights me up instantly. He's overjoyed at my perky condition. 'I've brought you some fruit, you look great. You're beautiful. You're glowing, my darling.'

'It's all these bloody X-rays I've been having.' We natter for half an hour, then he settles down to watch the news and finish off the grapes.

He makes me feel gifted and special and safe. I doze off. He creeps out.

Sleep like a log, interrupted now and again for blood pressure and temperature and to replace the saline. The sound of retching orchestrates each waking. Poor devils. Why not me? Perhaps it has an accumulative effect, perhaps the BOM part of the treatment will make me ill, perhaps tomorrow, perhaps never. I'm drifting off to sleep feeling great and wondering where the lions are.

17

Monday 13 February

BOM day. Lashing rain has flattened itself against the windows, turning the Constable outside into a Monet. I feel terrific and while Kenneth fetches the newspapers I have a leisurely bath.

If anything, I feel better than I did before I started chemotherapy (**it's early days**). No sickness, no diarrhoea, no tiredness; in fact, due to the steroids, my energy levels are *up*.

We don't have any full-length mirrors in the cottage as yet, but the shaving mirror reflects a rounder face than I'm expecting. (**Perhaps you're looking through the magnified side.**) It's the steroids again. I'm sure I've gained weight. I don't have any bathroom scales – I've been 8 stone 4 lbs most of my life, why have a machine to tell me something I already know? I'll weigh myself at the hospital when I get there.

I seldom walk around naked (**you look like scaf-**

folding) as I'm a little self-conscious, but Kenneth walks in and tells me I'm beautiful, and for a while I believe him. After four years of marriage, he's still tossing bouquets.

We met in the BBC canteen (**how romantic.**) *I was filming 'Hillary', a T.V. sit-com, and Kenneth was editing* Huis Clos *– a play he'd just directed with Omar Sharif and Jeanne Moreau. I was standing in the lunch queue in dressing-gown and curlers watching Brutus trying to stab a gherkin.*

Cliff Richard was rearranging lettuce at the cold table in search of a crispy bit and a Roman soldier in front of me ordered a chicken curry 'without that hot yellow gravy'. Philip Madoc, who played my boss in the series, stopped en route to the pudding queue and said: 'Mart, I'm dining with a friend who'd like to be introduced to you. Will you stop by my table as you leave the canteen?'

I said I would and burgers and chips in hand, returned to the gossip round the make-up girls' table. The gossip was so absorbing, I forgot Philip's invitation and, on leaving the canteen, wandered towards his attention-catching wave, wondering what he wanted.

He rose to greet me.

'Marti, I'd like you to meet Kenneth Ives.' And I turned into the sun and shook hands with a huge featureless silhouette.

Later, during a break in rehearsals, Philip asked me what I thought of him.

'Who?'

'Kenneth Ives.'

'Well, I didn't really have time to form an opinion and I couldn't see his face, the sun was in my eyes.'

'He's going to ring you and ask you out to dinner, and he's asked me to put a word in for him – watch him, he's a

womaniser!'

I adore Philip, he's bliss to work with and has an impish sense of humour. 'A fine recommendation, Philip!' And it was. I like men who like women.

Our conversation was interrupted by an A.F.M. who said there was a Mr Ives on the phone and did I wish to take the call?

Grinning at Philip, I walked through to the office and picked up the receiver to hear a cultured, 'Kenneth Ives. I was wondering whether you would consider having dinner with me?'

'Yes. When?' (I'm glad you didn't sound too eager.) I needed all the rehearsal time I could get, and didn't have any to squander, pussy-footing around with niceties. A date was arranged for the following evening.

In the coffee break, Philip gave me some background. He'd first met Kenneth in 1971 when he'd played Magua to Kenneth's Hawkeye for the B.B.C. I remembered watching it with the kids and formed a vague recollection of a tall man in buckskins and a Davy Crockett hat.

They'd worked together again in 'Poldark', by which time Kenneth had made a career move to become '... a brilliant director, National Theatre, Harold Pinter, Strindberg ...' Out of my league.

' ... and remember he's a bit of a lad.'

The 'bit of a lad' was five minutes late, and from my vantage point in the coffee shop I scanned the foyer of the Kensington Hilton, my home for the duration of the show, looking for a Davy Crockett hat.

The clatter of cutlery stopped for a second while everyone's attention was riveted to a tall, compelling figure striding through the coffee shop. He stopped at my chair, 6 feet 4 inches of shoulders swathed in a dramatic black overcoat, with elegant white beard and blue eyes. I was stunned by his enormous presence and sat open-mouthed, wondering who he was. (Isn't this the 'someday' you were expecting your prince to come?)

'Hello. Sorry I'm late, the car's on double yellows, do you like Indian?' It was him.

I was fancying Japanese actually, but didn't have the breath to say so as my prince grabbed an arm and hoisted me across the foyer and through the doors to his valiant steed, panting at the kerb in the shape of an immaculate '66 Mercedes Coupe. The man had style.

Two days later, on our third date, he proposed: 'I love you in that hat, will you marry me?'

'I can't Wednesday, I'm washing my hair.'

'Leave the arrangements to me.' (God, but he's masterful.) and I floated off to Birmingham to begin rehearsals for the nine-week 'Cannon & Ball Christmas Show'.

We conducted a brief, equidistant courtship at the Bear in Woodstock and six weeks after our first meeting, were married at Birmingham Register Office in the presence of two witnesses – Pam and Philip Madoc – along with Kenneth's sister and brother-in-law and the entire British media. It's been a fascinating marriage of contrast, a perfect example of opposites attract – our first tiff was because he scoffed when he realised I didn't know that Othello was black (and he didn't know that Stevie Wonder was).

We arrived at the Cromwell Hospital in time for our 10 o'clock appointment and followed the same procedure as last week: down to the basement for a blood test and cannula fitting, then up to the chemo ward on the third floor, where I climbed into 'jamas and bed and waited.

Kenneth shared coffee and sandwiches before leaving me to it, and Ludi – alias 'Philippino Smile' – came in with her tray of goodies and after my relaxation routine began to administer the BOM part of the treatment.

A large syringe of bleomycin, followed by a small one of oncovin, then a mixture of methotrexate and saline from a litre drip-bag, followed by six pints of saline to wash it through. I was amazed to discover last week that an intravenous drip is quite painless. It's easy to forget it's there, and several times I stretched the drip-pipe to its limit in pursuit of an out-of-reach object.

So far, the worst part of the treatment was boredom, and I walked around the room dragging my reluctant drip-stand behind me. It was like taking a cat for a walk on a lead. They must have nicked the casters from a supermarket trolley; it went everywhere but with me.

My boredom was relieved by brief, chirpy visits from nurses and staff and Dr McKenzie, who was surprised and pleased to find me seemingly unaffected by the usual side effects. His probing fingers confirmed what I already knew – the lumps were noticeably smaller.

He explained that methotrexate was a highly caustic poison and an antidote or 'rescue' of folinic acid had to be administered after precisely 24 hours or death would probably occur. (Now he tells you.) To ensure the poison is neutralised, the rescue is backed up with folinic acid tablets, taken every six of the next 48 hours, after which a blood test tells you how effective the antidote has been.

The immune system is at a very low ebb and he warned me to keep away from crowds – particularly children – as I'm susceptible to infection, and to discontinue my hobbies of gardening and carpentry as a scratch could lead to septicaemia.

After Kenneth's visit, I watched the 'in-house' movie

and snuggled down for an early night with the usual interruptions for blood pressure and temperature checks. At around 4 a.m. the need to empty my bladder necessitated several minutes of manoeuvring as I tried to persuade my drip-stand to follow me to the bathroom.

No sooner was I seated than a violent and explosive attack of diarrhoea took me by surprise (**now you know why they call it BOM**) and I spent ten minutes on my hands and knees with a bottle of TCP – which I always carry in my soap-bag – cleaning up the embarrassing evidence. The chemicals burnt my bum, but a quick bath solved the problem and I was back in bed before anyone noticed my absence.

Thursday 16 February

Because I had to wait for the 24-hour rescue, I stayed in hospital for an extra day, which I spent answering the mail that was still coming in from Cambridge. I was delighted when Kenneth collected me from the Cromwell and drove me home to the cottage, where I set my alarm and faithfully took my rescue tablets every six hours. I felt fine this morning as I readied myself for the blood level test back at the Cromwell. I took an unprovoked bite at Kenneth's ankles. I can't understand why. (**Must look up 'Chemotherapy and the Emotions'.**)

Dr McKenzie found my blood levels were almost back to normal. I've made an amazingly fast recovery (**it's the beef tea**) and up to now have experienced none of the usual chemotherapy side effects apart from white cracks – methotrexate burns – at the corners of my mouth. (**The hair's O.K., but the lips are falling off.**) I also mentioned my increasing lack of tolerance and libido. I seem to be off sex for the first time since discovering it.

My first sexual experience was a 'ménage-à-trois' with the boy next door and a dog.

It was the dog's fault. He was a wire-haired terrier called Buster, a present from my Dad just before he died. The dog was uncontrollable and would attack anything on four legs. He travelled miles hanging from the throat of any passing Alsatian that took his fancy. Once off the lead it would take a fortnight to get him back. Consequently, when we moved to Scotland he spent most of his life tied up in my Scots Grandmother's empty chicken hut.

It was a nice hut, dark and warm and, despite a permanently open skylight, still rich with the aroma of incontinent chickens. On hot summer afternoons I'd spend my time playing house, happily alone except for Buster, who was glad of the company. One day he started doing strange things to my leg. I was fascinated by the bright pink appendage that suddenly appeared and touched it with wonder. Buster liked it a lot, and would no doubt have died of exhaustion by the end of the summer had it not been for the boy next door, who had been spying through the skylight and threatened to tell my Grandmother unless I did the same to him. I ran. The dog died of loneliness, and for all I know the boy next door is still on the roof of the chicken hut.

I've never had much luck with either pets or men since.

Blackie the cat for instance. He was a kitten when I was, and I would dress him in doll's clothes lovingly knitted by my Nan. The leggings went on first. These restricted his movements and gave some protection against the viciously scrabbling hindquarters, and, with a strategically cut hole for his tail to come through, he looked quite cute. The bonnet came next. He really hated that bonnet. It flattened his ears and made him look like a monkey. Being vain, he'd growl and snort in outraged indignation. Once threaded and buttoned into the little jacket his wardrobe was complete. Then came the best bit.

With a few feet of broad elastic riffled from my Nan's famous button-box, I would strap him to the mattress of my doll's pram, with his spitting, bonneted head on a dainty pillow, and his thrashing tail neatly restricted within tucked-in blankets. Then I let the whole shebang career down the five steps leading from the front door across the path, across the drive and smack to a sudden stop against a low dividing wall. Cat and mattress would catapult out and land in next door's iris patch. After that the cat cleverly avoided me.

I digress – back to the dirty bit.

Boys cleverly avoided me until I was fourteen. On their return to school after the six-week holidays, they discovered I'd grown boobs, and none of 'em ever looked me in the eye again.

I didn't have many boy-friends, my Pop being sufficient deterrent for most young hopefuls. In my last year of school, I was a Saturday girl for British Home Stores, where I was courted for a while by a shy 21-year-old stockroom worker called Doug. He was on 'management training', and though he never so much as held my hand, once wrote an innocent love letter that concluded with a quote from Romeo and Juliet:

> Sleep dwell upon thine eyes,
> Peace in thy breast.
> Would I were sleep and peace,
> So sweet to rest.

And my Pop hit him for writing dirty letters.

After the dog and before my divorce from Malc, there was no one else – an attempt at a retaliatory affair was spotted on day one by Malc and brought to an unconsummated end on day *three. After our divorce, I was amazed to find I had no confidence sexually, and the thought of taking my clothes off in front of a strange man was out of the question. Cosmopolitan magazine had assured me that in 'seeking oneself after divorce, a woman often indulged in mild promiscuity. I remained unfound until my trip to Africa in 1981. I was free, I told myself. What was I waiting for? So far I'd slick-mouthed my way out of all approaches. I'd been in Sun City for six weeks now. The twelve performances per week left Sunday evening and all of Monday free. I left the Sunday night disco bar and a warm Coke, feeling angry with myself for demolishing yet another contender.*

A large American: 'I got two hundred and ten pounds o' muscle for you, babe.'

'And two ounces of brain. Say good night, Gracie!'

Octagonal glass pods slid up and down the outside of the main hotel ferrying people up to the top fourth floor and down to the sub-basement and pool exit – the quickest way back to my villa.

What had happened to romance? How did one 'pull' and remain a lady? I waited, mulling over the problem behind three American ladies who were shouting to be heard over the rattle of their diamond and gold jewellery.

The lift descends, the doors open and there he is. A charcoal-grey Armani with brilliant white shirt and matching teeth; a six foot two suntan with grey temples and green eyes that say 'WANT' and he pins me to the wall with them as I squeeze in behind the three ladies.

Down to the basement; two ladies get out, one man gets in. Sub-basement. My stop? His stop? No, the man and woman get out, he stays in – so do I, and we're joined by the entire Rustenburg cub-scout movement. Back up to the basement and the doors open and close on the same occupants; ground floor disgorges the cubs and ingests a host of tiny Japanese businessmen (a con-

vention of garden gnomes) who ride with us to the mezzanine Galaxy Bar, where they are replaced by four austere Germans in their pool-side uniforms of towelling robes and slippers.

All the way up to the fourth floor his eyes keep me pinned, while the Germans 'Ach' and 'Phoomph' over the realisation that the pool is in a downward direction.

Down again, still pinned, past third to stop on second where he steps out and holds the door, waiting for me, his head on one side. (Go on, dozy mare, move!) I join him.

He takes my arm and propels me down the lush rose-lit corridor, the carpeted silence broken only by the chick-chick-chick of his room key, which he slides in with an erotic slowness.

The immaculate suite is lit only with mellow lamps by the six-foot bed and still silent, he slips out of his jacket, loosens his bow-tie and begins to undo his cufflinks, looking at me while I stand wondering what to do next.

I am wearing a white wraparound silk jersey dress, shoes and Balenciaga's 'Quadrille'. If I start disrobing now, I will be starkers before he reaches his shoelaces. I wait and watch while he finishes undressing and much as I would like to see what fate has in store for me, I dare not drag my eyes away from his.

He moves towards me, loosens the single hook on my dress and it slides to the floor.

I found myself that night – several times – and not a word was spoken.

I never saw him again.

I had read somewhere that the dimension of the male reproductive organ is directly proportionate to the size of his ears. There followed a few big-eared disappointments, before I settled down with a gentle Swiss lover who called me Shatzi and allowed me to thrash him at squash.

There aren't too many straight, single men of my own age around; pickings were thin. I can count my foreign affairs on one *hand and wouldn't dream of naming the famous (if only because there weren't any.)*

I returned to England and celibacy, having learned from my 'self-seeking' that sex was like smoking – if you have to stop, stop altogether, otherwise you could end up smoking everybody's.

18

Sunday 26 February
Week Three

Last Monday's chemotherapy was plain sailing with no apparent side effects. My hair remained firmly in place and my weight, which rose six pounds after the first treatment, is holding steady at 8 stone 10 lbs. I am hyperactive, thanks to a daily 25mg of prednisolone, a steroid which is also responsible for my lengthening nails and shortening temper.

Dr McKenzie is delighted – and amazed – at my tolerance to chemo. I tell him about my pre-chemo relaxation routine and my visualisation techniques. (**He probably thinks you're crackers.**) He doesn't scoff. He is convinced that relaxation is the key to cushy chemo.

Relaxing isn't as easy as one would imagine. I've read books which instructed me to let myself go 'heavy', starting at my ankles and working upwards to my head. For me, it works better the other way around – there's more tension in my head, neck and shoulders – and after half a dozen deep slow breaths – inhaling to capacity, then emptying the lungs completely – I let my tongue and jaw go slack (**not a pretty sight**). The scalp, cheeks and eyes relax automatically, once the tongue is relaxed. Then I concentrate on my throat and shoulders and downwards till I reach my feet, breathing normally through my nose, but concentrating on the 'out' breath, getting heavier and heavier. It's difficult not to fall asleep, but I make a point of doing it three times a day, before my visualisation and ALWAYS immediately before chemo.

I put my visualisation beavers to work during chemo as well. I have a 'Dad's Army' of flat-footed, short-sighted misfits (**a bit like the Tetley Tea men**) who, dressed in wellies, white overalls and a variety of headgear and armed with brushes and hose-pipes, march through my veins sluicing and sweeping all the dead cancer cells down gratings which lead to the purifying plant in my kidneys before they are disposed of through the normal channels.

My Royal Marine beavers have been busy hunting the fish-egg cancer cells, gobbling them up with glee until the three-minute warning tells them to return to camp – the marrow in my spine – as the allies are sending in Rentokil with poisonous chemicals. My beavers scurry to the trap-doors in my spine, climb inside and batten down the hatches, to recuperate and wait out the chemical invasion which destroys all dividing cells, including them if they don't get home in time.

One or two of my beavers don't make it and perish, and as soon as the 'all clear' sounds, my 'Dad's Army' sets out to clean the passage-ways, hosing the ceilings and walls and scouring every nook and cranny to oust the dead enemy. Once rested and refreshed, my Royal Marine beavers can't wait to dart once more into the fray and start to emerge even before the allies send in the folinic acid rescue that neutralises the poison; they're tough and resilient and most survive the lethal methotrexate.

My sister-in-law Maureen, and many of the letters I have received, recommend the Bristol Clinic, so Kenneth made an appointment and we drove over on Wednesday.

The Bristol Cancer Help Centre is housed in a converted convent and an air of peace and tranquillity still pervades. We met with Dr Michael Wetzler who explained the holistic approach, which includes self-help techniques such as stress control, positive visualisation, healing, relaxation, meditation and counselling on how to cope with emotions.

The patient books in for a week. It's a charitable organisation available to everyone, and has a fund to cover the costs for those unable to pay. The first part of the programme is diet – vegetarian and mostly raw, organically grown whenever possible, without salt, sugar or stimulants, and an individually designed vitamin/mineral supplement programme.

Dr Wetzler led Kenneth and me to the dining room to sample the delights of raw cuisine. It was highly palatable and much appreciated by the apparently contented late lunchers. Our brief visit confirmed that it is indeed a highly commendable organisation, but I decide not to take up any of the Bristol Clinic's valuable but limited space. As we left, we both felt heartened by the experience.

Pam and Eric came for the weekend, which we

spent chatting and flopping around for the most part. I was amazed when Pam decided to accompany Kenneth and Eric on a walk. Walking is something she usually only does as far as her Mercedes 300 SL and back. I watched with interest as she wafted upstairs to change into walking shoes which turned out to be four-inch Jordan stilettoes.

'Don't you have any sensible shoes?' demanded a wellingtoned Kenneth.

'These are sensible, Kenneth, I got them in the sale.' She strode past him, leaving him to follow her perfume.

It was a smashing weekend, just what I needed, and I was surprised how tired I was when they left. I deduced my energy levels must be dropping, which surprised me. I'd been fooled by the short bursts of steroid-induced hyperactivity. The expected happened unexpectedly, just before they left. I ran my hand through my hair and came away with a fist-full. (**You've still got more than Kenneth.**) Oddly enough, it didn't bother me but, though she didn't give any outward signs, I could feel Pam's distress.

Week Four
Sunday 5 March

My fourth treatment – BOM week – and due, I'm sure, to the relaxation, I experienced no sickness and felt fine when Kenneth picked me up on Wednesday morning to drive me home.

He had some meetings in town, so dropped me off at the London flat. Since Sunday, 90 per cent of my hair had come out, evenly, leaving an uncontrollable wispy covering. I decided to get rid of it and walked round to Queensway and into a salon. Removing my turban and hat, I asked the surprised hairdresser to shave my head, which he did in about five minutes. It looked much better, gave me a sort of 'athletic' look.

I had a luncheon appointment with Andy Taylor, M.D. of Central T.V. and Tony Wolfe, Head of Light Entertainment, to discuss my future. We met at the English House Restaurant, where I openly envied Andy's choice of bangers and mash, although my own meal was excellent. The conversation eventually turned to business and they very kindly offered me an hour of prime time for a 'special'. I couldn't have wished for anything better, and shall remember their loyalty and courage. Making expensive, long-term plans for someone with an uncertain future is very brave of them and provides me with yet another reason to succeed.

Since shooting to the middle after 'New Faces', my career continued to thrive for longer than my original estimate of three years. After 'The Summer Show' for the old A.T.V. network with other 'New Faces' acts, I was given my own six-week 'Marti' series and a ritzy Christmas special, before signing a three-year contract with the B.B.C. I stayed with the B.B.C. for the next seven years, doing cabaret and summer seasons between annual six-week series' of 'Marti' and a collection of specials.

When I returned from Africa, I needed a fresh challenge. The B.B.C. came up with the sit-com 'Hillary'. It was well received, I enjoyed acting and had made the transition successfully. Acting gave me a new avenue to explore and I accepted several plays at a basic repertory company wage, to widen my experience.

John got me a nine-week season in 'Funny Girl' at the

Crucible and Clare Venables, the director, didn't turn a hair when I read the part in a Yorkshire accent on day one. I learned more from Clare in a few short weeks than years of showbiz had taught me. She was my Svengali, and under her patient guidance I became a highly successful Fanny Brice. I will always love her for it.

I sensed a growing restlessness in John. He too needed a new challenge. In an attempt to scratch the itch, we'd invested in a health club, the brain-child of Sharon Somerset, a dynamic Northern business-woman ten years my junior. Within a few years — mostly due to her efforts — we had five successful clubs, and John's restlessness returned.

He was looking for the excitement he'd experienced on the day I'd won 'New Faces' and, despite the success of his new and long-established business ventures, he was disenchanted, like a man who knows he's had his finest hour.

Thanks to Clare Venables, I had decided to pursue acting and my own 'finest hour' which — though I've had some wonderful ones — I don't think I've had yet.

John knew nothing of the legitimate side of the business and, after finally persuading me to accept the first series of 'New Faces', we decided to drift apart to chase separate dreams. We parted amicably. He continues to possess the Midas touch and his newest departure into snooker clubs is a dazzling success.

I eventually resigned from the board of Sherbert, the health club business, as it requires time and dedication, both of which I had in very short bursts. Sharon and her man, Kevan, worked seven 18-hour days a week and, I felt, were rightfully entitled to the rewards.

My fairy godmother took a hand once more and I stumbled across the best agent in London, Laurie Evans.

As I left the restaurant the proprietors, noting my appreciation of Andy's sausages, handed me a pound of foil-wrapped sausages to cook at home. (**Do they know what they're asking?**)

They nestled in the bottom of my handbag during a meeting with my publisher, who graciously accepted less than half of the promised manuscript. I find I'm beginning to lose concentration, but it sounds such a feeble excuse and I'm angry with myself.

I was due back at the Cromwell the next day for the all-important blood count, but we both thought the hour's drive to the country was worth it, so returned to the cottage. I burnt the sausages, and flying into a rage, threw them across the kitchen (**much to Kenneth's amusement**). My tantrums are out of character and are becoming more frequent and always directed at Kenneth, who continues to bear them graciously. I can't find an explanation within the pages of the many books I've read, and intend to mention the problem to Dr McKenzie when next I see him.

My throat felt a little sore when I went to bed on Wednesday night and on Thursday morning – blood-count day – the back of my throat was lined with tiny white blisters. The soles of my feet and the palms of my hands were itching too. I found it difficult to swallow initially, but it gradually became easier, and I was my usual chirpy self when I arrived at the Cromwell for my blood-count test.

My blood count was almost normal, much to Ludi's amazement. However, she was quite concerned about the burns at the back of my throat, and rang Dr McKenzie, who is at the Hammersmith Hospital on Thursdays. On his recommendation, she gave me several glass ampoules of folinic acid to use as a mouthwash and to dab on the corners of my mouth which are now quite badly burnt.

By Friday the burns had spread to the roof of my mouth and tongue, large blisters lined my throat and the inside of my cheeks and lips. It wasn't as bad as it sounds and swallowing became easier as the day wore on. I ate cool, soft foods – rice pudding, beef tea and creamed potatoes – no seasoning or hot sauce, and only hurt myself once when I tried to open my mouth wide enough to examine my injuries.

I got the shock of my life. The blisters hung like putrid yellow awnings, and only when I realised it was the bright sunset yellow Lucozade dye did the vision of septicaemia fade. The folinic acid mouthwash didn't seem to do much good, and I ran out of it before the blisters subsided.

By this evening the inside of my mouth is almost back to normal, but my soles and palms continue to itch and feel slimy when wet. Tomorrow is week five of the treatment (**almost half-way through**). How time flies, and it's what I've come to regard as the easier PACE part of the treatment.

Week Five
Sunday 12 March

Monday's PACE went as well as usual and I'm still displaying no side effects, except the burns. I continue to employ my Royal Marine beavers and flat-foot brigade, and I'm convinced it helps. My hair has almost completely gone now and I've taken to wearing large headscarves, tied like a ponytail at the back of the neck, with a hat on top. I also make more of my eyes and the look is quite pleasing. I don't feel the need to wear wigs. To be honest, it's nice not to have to spend hours drying, curling and lacquering. I know you're dying to know – it's the first question intimate friends ask, once over the shock of a bald me – what about pubic hair? Still intact, though the hair beneath my arms hasn't regrown since shaving two weeks ago; those on my legs **(groomed to perfection on the same day)** are very slow-growing and my brows and lashes are thinning, especially on the left side.

My biggest problem to date has worsened over the past few weeks. Haemorrhoids. **(Must you go into such intimate detail?)** I mention this only because, if these chronicles are to be helpful, they have to be honest and though not a common side effect, it is one some people experience. Stupid, misguided 'delicacy' had prevented me from mentioning the problem to Dr McKenzie, but the burns have affected all major orifices **(or is it 'orifi'?)** and make the problem an even more agonising one.

Dr McKenzie examined the offending parts and sent for the 'arsehole specialist', who bounded in with more enthusiasm than his specialisation merited and, using an array of excruciating metal contraptions, viewed the matter from closer quarters, ignoring my cheery 'Yoo-hoo!' when his eye drew level with the source of my discomfort.

He prescribed some pessaries and ointment and some hideous packets of 'fibre gel' which supposedly provides poetry in motion. He asked if I'd used pessaries before and had the grace to laugh at the old reply of: 'Yes, but for all the good they did, I may as well have shoved 'em up my arse!'

When Dr McKenzie arrived for his usual 6 o'clock

visit to my bedside on Monday evening, I mentioned my unreasonable temper tantrums and he explained that chemotherapy, at my age, *always* induces an early menopause, and my lack of control was probably part of it.

I asked if there was anything he wanted while I was shoplifting. He said not and recommended hormone replacement therapy after the chemo. It gave me a strange feeling, knowing my reproductive days were over (**consider yourself lucky. The menopause happened on a Wednesday**).

I have always been 'regular in my habits' as they say, a fact I've taken totally for granted and though I'm not – dare I say – constipated, the whole process is so excruciating that it takes an enormous effort of will to make myself relax and allow nature to take its course. The morning ritual leaves me weak and sweaty and the chemicals burn like acid. By Wednesday I realised that plunging into a ready-drawn bath immediately afterwards cuts down on the discomfort.

While we're on the subject, I tried the pessaries. After twenty minutes, with a pair of nail clippers and my dressmaking scissors, I managed to free the white waxy bullet-shaped pessary from its foil wrap and tried to follow the instructions: 'Insert'. So far, anything passing that particular sphincter has come from the other direction (**you're a virgin at last**) and the pessary was only marginally easier to get in than it was to get out.

By Thursday small white burnt patches had appeared on my hands and feet, as a result of the treatment before last. The chemicals must stay in the system a long time, and I'm curious as to why they should affect my extremities.

My weight remains at 8 stone 10 lbs, but the

steroids have made my face puffy (**on you it's an improvement**). My eyes and nose run persistently, which I think is a result of the chemicals. Apart from that – so far, so good.

19

**Week Six
Sunday 19 March**

Half-way house.

Before we left for the Cromwell Hospital and BOM on Monday, a team of builders arrived under the leadership of Ron Walker, the architect. The promise I made to myself is about to be fulfilled and the house renovated.

Over the years Ron has become a great friend. He taught me to see with fresh eyes. He gently guided me away from kitsch and gave me the courage to express my individuality. He planted a seed of awareness that grows each day and my interests expanded to include architecture and landscaping. The best gift he gave me was a love for gardening (which could become an obsession) and I yearn for the time when I can stay home long enough to control the mayhem that thrusts from my herbaceous borders on my return from a three-month session somewhere.

He is one of those fortunate men with a perfect wife (a Cordon Bleu nymphomaniac, who likes a drinking man?). Gill showed me the peaceful pleasure of flower arranging and tries not to laugh at my gradually improving efforts. They are faithful, undemanding friends – much valued. I consider them 'family'.

The soles of my feet were tender due to the burns, but apart from my 'Miss Piggy' slippers I have no flat shoes (I don't suppose the wellies go with the hat), so I gritted my teeth and hobbled across the gravel to the car in my ridiculous stilettoes.

The nursing team are now old friends and greet me warmly, admiring my outfit, which I try to vary each week for their appraisal. I always arrive in full slap, flash gear and as much spring in my step as I can muster; it fools the world and me as well.

After my usual ten-minute relaxation routine the BOM treatment was as easy as usual and resulted in no side effects. I've never had a repeat of the diarrhoea which accompanied the first BOM treatment, and when Dr McKenzie came to visit he told me he intended to start the folinic acid rescue six hours earlier to try to stop the burns which seem to pop up days after the treatment.

He also cut my steroids down by half to 12mg and warned me to expect changes in my energy levels. (Who the hell's going to clean the oven now?)

Nina Myskow bounced in to visit me on Monday. She's been a regular visitor since I started the treatment, and I must say she looked stunning. She'd lost a load of weight (she's in love at the moment) and was wearing a bright pink fitted jacket with a peplum and a short black skirt. Her eyes were sparkling, her skin glowing: in short, she looked beautiful and I experienced a rare prickling of envy.

She was bearing gifts of tofu, yogurt and other soft foods to accommodate my burnt mouth. She also brought a copy of *Swimming to Cambodia* (a change from your usual *Beano* and *Dandy*), but my lack of concentration continues to worsen, so I doubt I'll read it for some time.

Last week I watched the same video twice without realising, and still couldn't tell you what the film was about.

Despite the burns, my blood-count recovery rate is amazing and I feel quite well. My flashes of uncontrollable rage persist, and Kenneth still bears the brunt of it with dignity and grace. He fetches and carries and carts me about, pandering to my every whim only to be bruised by a barrage of abuse.

He does all the shopping and on Friday he brought home some plums which didn't meet with my approval. To my shame, I threw the plums at him, stamping my feet like a 3-year-old. It's not a side of myself that I've seen before. I don't like it, but try as I might I'm powerless against the moods. **(Perhaps it's a necessary release of suppressed anger.)** I tend to be self-analytical and trap myself into corners if not careful. Think I'll give in and just let it happen.

We had lunch with my T.V. producer, Richard Holloway, today. I've known his wife, Camilla, since my early T.V. days when she was one of my lovely dancers. She has now become a highly successful T.V. producer herself. The other guests include Keith Strachan, musical associate, his wife and David Hillier, who I'm hoping will direct the special planned for later this year. We had a lovely day and talked about everything but television.

The early rescue seems to be the answer to the burns problem. They are much improved and no new ones have emerged, as yet, after Monday's BOM.

Week Seven
Sunday 26 March

Another trouble-free treatment this week. Dr McKenzie now pops in just to be cheered up by my comparatively chirpy condition. He says he's never come across anyone quite as tolerant of chemo, and wishes I could bottle whatever it is that resists most of the usual awful side effects.

The haemorrhoids continue to be a problem, but less of one, and I'm getting hooked on the morning agony. I've noticed the steroid reduction. I have less energy and my limbs jerk involuntarily, especially at night.

My temper tantrums remained submerged over the weekend when Linda and Malc came to stay. The visit lifted my spirits and some of my old energy returned (which proves the importance of 'attitude').

Week Eight and Onwards

From here on the entries in my diary are scant. My concentration span became very short, and my thumbs and index fingers too burnt to hold a pencil.

My veins have become burnt and it has been difficult to find one which would accept a needle. That sounds much worse than it actually was. I was unaware that my veins were burnt, except for a slightly 'bruised' feeling, and the condition was more of a problem for the nurses than for me. I can honestly say I hardly ever felt a needle going in. The care and tenderness of the British medical profession is infinite. My gratitude is beyond words.

Several things remain constant: Kenneth's patience and selfless dedication; the daily support of my precious friends and family; the hammering and banging from the builders. Deprived of gardening and the odd sojourn into crowded places, I became restless and began to long for a holiday.

Pleasant events stand out in my memory. Visits from Walker to check on the building progress. Phone conversations with distant friends. Visits from dancers who long ago became friends. A pot of African violets which seemed to last for ever; they were a present from my sister-in-law Maureen, who always seems to buy the right gift. She rings most days; the concern of Kenneth's family has been overwhelming.

A visit to my agent, Laurence Evans, fortified me. Laurie is my mentor, the 'Grand Señor' of agents and a gentleman of the old school. He's a tall, dignified man of considerable maturity and wisdom, and a shrewd business-man – at least four steps ahead of the game, and indispensable. He would make an excellent subject for a biography with a clientele that reads like *Who's Who of the Theatre*: Sir Laurence Olivier, Sir John Mills, Sir Rex Harrison, Douglas Fairbanks, Albert Finney, Dame Wendy Hiller, Maggie Smith, Dinah Sheridan, Joan Plowright, Sir John Gielgud – and me. I don't even belong on the list. I'm like a Fourth Division goalie in the England net. I met him when Kenneth introduced us at a party given by Sir John and Lady Mills. We took to each other instantly and I like to think he added me to his prestigious list because he thinks I have talent. He's taught me a lot and laughs with delight at some of my *faux pas* at his star-studded parties.

I once told Maggie Smith she was wonderful in *The Rivals* when it had been Geraldine McEwan who played the part. I asked Sir Peter Hall what he did for a living. And on being introduced to a sparky old gent, felt foolish when he answered, 'OLIVIER, dear,' to my, 'Larry who?'

Since marrying Kenneth, the odd social gathering is often peopled with lords, ladies and politicians as well as the above-mentioned stars, and I've found myself sitting next to Glenda Jackson, chatting to Lauren Bacall or treading on the toes of Charlton Heston. I try not to embarrass Kenneth with my social inadequacies. I no longer refer to a napkin as a serviette, a lavatory as a toilet, or Baryshnikov as Barry Snekoff, and I've learned that Epstein did a bit of sculpting when he wasn't managing the Beatles.

After visiting Laurie, I felt so good I decided to go to the Conran shop. I know I was told to keep away from the risk of infection, but I was high on freedom and the day was lovely. I began to feel weak and light-headed after walking round the shop for five minutes, and had to sit in the coffee shop until I had the strength to flag a cab and return to the flat.

It made me realise that chemotherapy has had a devastating effect on my body, even though I have a high tolerance. It's frightening and frustrating. I've always taken my abundant energy for granted. I could easily be pulled down by the quicksand of self-pity and only just succeeded in pushing away the fear with positive thought. (Drastic disease requires drastic treatment. Of course you feel a bit weak, but according to Dr McKenzie you're better off than anyone he's ever known after nine weeks of chemo. Only three to go, soon you'll begin to feel better. You'll have beaten it, you can begin a keep-fit programme, your hair will grow, you have an exciting future. You'll win, I promise.)

I borrowed a keep-fit video from Nina and watched Callan Pinkney do callanetics for hours (I'm sure it's firmed up your eyeballs).

An extraordinary thing happened in week ten. A phone call just before chemo robbed me of the time for relaxation, and I experienced the vomiting and shaking – called rigor – for the first time. On weeks eleven and twelve I did the usual ten-minute relaxation and so avoided any repeat of the sickness. Relaxation works!

After my final treatment a scan confirmed I was in remission. Some nodes remained in various places – groin, armpit, diaphragm – but were greatly reduced, and my spleen was no longer enlarged. A second scan was booked for a month later. I felt fine, if a little disappointed – I thought I'd be completely clear.

The soles of my feet and my finger-ends were very sore for the first few days after my last treatment, and it looks as though I'll lose a few nails. The good news is the hairs on my legs are beginning to grow, and so are my eyelashes. There doesn't seem to be any regrowth on my head as yet, and my tenacious but thinning pubendum looks like the last of the Mohicans. My eyes and nose continue to run, my face is still puffy despite the fact that my steroids have now been reduced to 6mg daily, and my weight remains constant at 8 stone 10lbs. I've noticed long, thin, brown lines like claw-marks running up my arms and across my shoulders. Dr McKenzie says they're pigmentation marks, caused by the chemo, and while the hair will grow back I'm stuck with the pigmentation marks (**proudly borne battle scars**).

When we arrived home after my last chemo, tragic news awaited us. Pam's Dad had died suddenly and without warning. It was a dreadful shock for them; Cyril was always such a healthy man, easygoing and consistently good-natured. I vividly remember first meeting him at Pam's sixth birthday party. They had a bright red kitchen and Cyril opened the door to me and said: 'Ah do, Lini-Pin, welcome to t'fire station.' He continued to call me Lini-Pin for the rest of his life. The last time I'd seen him was during my pre-chemo visit to Sheffield. He was hoeing round some daffodils in Pam's magnificent garden and said: 'Ah do, Lini-Pin. Welcome to t'Chelsea Flower Show.' At his funeral, I didn't know what to do or say to ease Pam's grief. She adored him.

Pam's mom is bearing up well, but I worry about her. Thelma has been a surrogate mother to me and always handled life's ups, downs and emergencies with calm, competent efficiency. Often, she'd babysit our four collective kids – all under two years old - without turning a hair. Hiding beneath her Yorkshire accent lies a sharp intelligence. Under different circumstances, she could easily have gone to university, and her wisdom and advice is widely sought, but I sense a great fragility and feel the burden of constantly being seen to 'cope' is getting to her.

The second scan on May 24th showed further reduction of the cancerous tissue, proving remission is still in progress. If this continues over the next five months, I have a 50 per cent chance of being cured. My eyes and nose continue to run, but my face is less puffy, and I am now off the steroids completely after cutting down from 6mg per day to 6mg every *other* day.

A barely visible covering of downy fluff now covers my head, and all other parts are growing with a vengeance. My weight remains constant but, as yet, my energy and concentration span are limited. I find it very frustrating and after failing to do more than two or three repetitions of Nina's exercise tape, found myself falling into a pit of despair. (**Dr McKenzie warned you. You won't begin to feel better for quite a while. The chemicals stay in the system for months, continuing to destroy any remaining enemies. Have a little patience, woman!**)

A holiday in Corfu made me look better, but I didn't feel too energetic and still lacked the concentration to pursue my holiday habit of avid reading. Instinct told me to keep out of the sun, and I confined my exposure to an hour in the late afternoons.

Towards the middle of the second week, history repeated itself. I was applying some Factor 4 when I discovered a lump under my right arm. Oh, my God! It's come back. (**Calm down, calm down. You have layman's fingers and a vivid imagination. For that very reason you never examine yourself for lumps. For all you know it could be scar tissue, it's very, very small, wait and see what Dr McKenzie has to say.**) I decided there and then that I would go in for the bone marrow transplant should my suspicions prove correct.

Once again Dr McKenzie allayed my fears. It was merely scar tissue, which he felt was even more reduced than when last he examined me, but it made me realise how near to the surface my fear lies.

20

Monday 25 September

It's a year – almost to the day – since a biopsy confirmed I had terminal lymph cancer. We're early for my appointment with Dr McKenzie. He has the results of my latest scan, and by now he'll know whether the months of chemo have had the desired effect.

The subtle luxury of the Cromwell Hospital waiting area envelops a cosmopolitan clientele and – save for the whispered conversations common to all waiting rooms – could be the lounge of an international five-star hotel.

Kenneth clears his throat loudly, absorbed behind his *Times,* and a young Arab stops picking his nose long enough to look up and see what the noise is. He sits with three others, identically costumed in kaftan, headdress and Marks and Spencer socks. The import duty on their Rolexes would pay the National Debt, and I'm mesmerised by the flashing diamonds on his nose-picking fingers as the young Arab continues to plumb the far reaches.

Two scrawny parchment ladies walk past, over-sunned and stretch-faced in Valentino and patent pumps, with plum hair severely drawn back from widow's peaks into petersham-ribboned ponytails.

Four pairs of liquid-brown eyes watch, safe between yashmak and hood, and tinkling gold bracelets highlight their giggles hidden behind henna-flowered hands.

Fat Greek women spill from fat armchairs and one leans over to admonish a fat grey grandson who sprawls sulking on the pale carpet behind her chair.

Three Philippino cleaners, crisp and pretty in off-duty clothes, chatter past and wave to me, en route to their secret lives; a Turkish gentleman, a carp with hooded eyes, regards my legs frankly.

A couple step out of a consulting room, followed by a tall, ascetic specialist. He stands between them, cloaking them with his arms, and bends his head to speak earnestly to first one and then the other. They don't hear him. They share the familiar glazed expression of shock and despair. Tears glisten from the edge of dark pits beneath the woman's sunken eyes, and her face is so gaunt I think at first it must be her, but the wispy patches of hair clinging to the man's head prove *him* to be the victim.

Anger blazes from the man's puffy face and I wonder how I'll react if *my* news is bad. I've never considered the possibility before this moment. My hair has grown back – wavy and grey! (**I don't understand, it was straight and purple when it fell out.**) I feel stronger every day. I'm working like the clappers on my T.V. special, and have almost forgotten I was ill (**it doesn't do to become complacent!**). Perhaps I should prepare myself for bad news, but how? (**If it's failed, you've** merely lost the first skirmish, we've still got the bone marrow transplant.) At least I can rely on Dr McKenzie to tell me the truth. I've always insisted on it; perhaps in some cases ignorance is bliss, but not for me.

It's my body, how can I fight if I don't know what I'm invaded by? (And if you've only got a short time, why not run amok on your American Express? Build up your children's character – bequeath them your over-draft.)

I've had the opportunity to meet the *truly* brave: a laughing, legless seven-year-old boy; a pale, quiet Scottish kid, cheerfully losing her hair for the second time after the first chemo failed to control her leukaemia; a beautiful fifteen-year-old girl who said: 'That's O.K., I wanna live,' when they told her they had to amputate her leg.

Cancer has worked *for* me. It's renewed old acquaintances and banished old grievances, rearranged my priorities and quelled imagined needs. It's diluted my greed and strengthened my resolve, opened my mind and forced me to take an earnest look at my life and myself. It's not all nice, but I'm learning to live with the things I can't change and, on the whole, I like myself.

Dr McKenzie's beautiful Philippino nurse, Bijou, is smiling at me from behind reception. She waves before collecting a file and walking towards us.

'How are you? Your hair! Wow – isn't it thick, looks very good, suits you – and how are you keeping, Mr Ives? Well, I hope. Dr McKenzie will see you now, Mrs Ives,' and we follow her to the small consulting room.

I marvel once again at the compassionate care and concern from overworked medical staff; their dedication is absolute, whether National Health or posh private, though I'll admit to a preference for posh private (**why not throw up in luxury?**) and am extremely grateful for my medical insurance. The B.C.W.A. has been extremely helpful and accommodating. (**If this is the advertising section, I think John Lewis, Marks and Spencer, British Airways and Central T.V. deserve a mention.**)

Dr McKenzie smiles up from his notes and stops writing for a moment. I think I'm a little in love with him (**that's normal according to Barbara Cartland**).

'Hello. Take a seat, I won't be long,' and he continues to write while I gaze at the through section X-rays of myself back-lit on the wall. Eventually he finishes and sits back smiling, while recapping his fountain pen.

'Well, now! The scan confirms what my fingers told me. You are still in remission. There's still a little scar tissue, but it's much reduced, your pancreas is normal and while we can never say you're completely cured, you stand more than a 50 per cent chance.' (**That's a big leap from no chance at all.**)

The longer I stay in remission, the greater my chances of survival, and I won't allow fear of its return to shadow my life. Should it dare come back, I'm ready for it; I'm not intimidated any more, I know it's beatable. Tales of tragedy fuel our fear and stay vivid longer than success stories, but the fact remains that cancers *are* curable and doctors can tell of an increasing number of 'miraculous' and unaccountable recoveries made by patients diagnosed as 'terminally ill'. Ordinary people, not blessed with special powers or extra-strong wills, survive against the odds because they're not prepared to surrender without a struggle.

Not for a second did I ever believe I would die (**even**

though you know you're a head-burying dreamer?). I know I'm not a realist, but my sense of tomorrow is so vivid, I have such a lot to finish and start and besides, I haven't had my finest hour.

Life has taught me that most blessings come in disguise, and with my newly heightened perception I already recognise my brush with cancer as another. If you are a sufferer, you may think that a shade incredible, but hear me out.

In the past year I've lost a few nails, a lot of hair and a little vanity. All are growing back with a vengeance and my gains are many and precious. I know time will rob me of the glow of these newly-gotten gains and soon they'll be tarnished by complacency, so I'll pen them while I still see the colours.

The last year has added ten years' experience to my young marriage. Kenneth and I have seen sides of each other that might never have come to light. It's brought us closer faster, and I thank God for him.

My sons have matured with merit from the experience and my respect for them has grown. I can now view them as people rather than sons, and I have discovered I *like* them as well as love them.

My friends have never been so important to me. I've never allowed myself the luxury of needing anyone before, and it was a wonderful revelation when I realised I did. They are there at any time of the day or night, prepared to drop what they are doing and fly to my side with support ranging from spiritual to financial. I feel an almost tangible umbilical link, as if we're a part of the same ancient family, and know we're irrevocably bonded.

I always thought the planet beautiful, thought

myself sensitive to nature, leaving no trace of myself on the landscape, trying not to crush life with a careless footfall and resisting the urge to pick flowers for fear of hearing them scream. Since becoming aware of my mortality, the world has changed to technicolour and I'm in awe at the wonder of it all. There's something eternal about a mighty tree, something inspiring about a slender solitary weed thrusting for life through concrete. I'm surrounded by survival, despite the odds, and my own determination is renewed.

My faith in humanity has been restored. As well as the thousands of caring letters I've received, people are constantly coming up to me and wishing me well. Their concern has been genuine and has kept my spirits high. They have lent me courage by calling me 'brave', so I pretend I am because I don't want to let them down, and sometimes I manage to fool myself as well.

Sometimes I catch sight of my mother in myself, the way I move my head, the shape of my hands, an odd expression; and it frightens me. I'm so like her in many ways and yet so different. She could never accept responsibility for her own condition, blaming everyone and everything. I have discovered we are all responsible for our *own* failures and successes. You either hide from the dragon or square up and fight and in the end the expression 'If it is to be, it is up to me!' is proven beyond doubt. Things are never as bad as they seem, once you decide to face your problem. Fight – no matter the odds – what have you got to lose?

I always knew this particular story would have a happy ending, but even if it hadn't it would still be a success story because I finally conquered the real enemy – fear.